W9-CNM-335

"Don't even think about it, truck. I stupidly agreed to direct a play we're to put on in three months— with no lead actor. I have no time to tinker with your engine."

"Excuse me?"

Dani studied the handsome man before her. He had the kind of smile you immediately trusted, which was exactly why she kept up her guard. Hadn't she learned the hard way that nothing was as it seemed?

She thought she knew everyone in town, but she didn't know him. But then she had a flickering memory of a church potluck dinner given to welcome Blessing's newest doctor.

"Yes, Dr. Duke?"

"Um, actually, it's Luc. Lucas Lawrence. Did you need something?"

Dr. Duke—no, Luc—was perfect for the lead, the answer to her prayers.

Books by Lois Richer

Love Inspired

LOIS RICHER

Sneaking a flashlight under the blankets, hiding in a thicket of Caragana bushes where no one could see, pushing books into socks to take to camp—those are just some of the things Lois Richer freely admits to in her pursuit of the written word. "I'm a book-a-holic. I can't do without stories," she confesses. "It's always been that way."

Her love of language evolved into writing her own stories. Today her passion is to create tales of personal struggle that lead to triumph over life's rocky road. For Lois, a happy ending is essential.

"In my stories, as in my own life, God has a way of making all things beautiful. Writing a love story is my way of reinforcing my faith in His ultimate goodness toward us—His precious children."

HEAVEN'S KISS

LOIS RICHER

Published by Steeple Hill Books™

If you purchased this book without a cover you should be aware
that this book is stolen property. It was reported as "unsold and
destroyed" to the publisher, and neither the author nor the
publisher has received any payment for this "stripped book."

 STEEPLE HILL BOOKS

Steeple
Hill®

ISBN 0-373-87247-X

HEAVEN'S KISS

Copyright © 2004 by Lois Richer

All rights reserved. Except for use in any review, the reproduction
or utilization of this work in whole or in part in any form by any
electronic, mechanical or other means, now known or hereafter
invented, including xerography, photocopying and recording, or in
any information storage or retrieval system, is forbidden without
the written permission of the editorial office, Steeple Hill Books,
233 Broadway, New York, NY 10279 U.S.A.

All characters in this book have no existence outside the imagination of
the author and have no relation whatsoever to anyone bearing the same
name or names. They are not even distantly inspired by any individual
known or unknown to the author, and all incidents are pure invention.

This edition published by arrangement with Steeple Hill Books.

® and TM are trademarks of Steeple Hill Books, used under license.
Trademarks indicated with ® are registered in the United States Patent
and Trademark Office, the Canadian Trade Marks Office and in other
countries.

Visit us at www.steeplehill.com

Printed in U.S.A.

We know the love that God has for us,
and we trust that love. God is love.
Those who live in love live in God,
and God lives in them.

—1 *John* 4:16

This book is dedicated to those who in struggling
to do the ordinary, accomplish the extraordinary.
Mom, teachers, doctors, preachers—
the list covers many. You know who you are.
God bless you.

Prologue

What a way to begin the second month of a new year.

"Okay, let me get this straight. My father wanted me to have the ranch, to keep the Double D running." Dani DeWitt waited for the lawyer's nod.

"Yes. Dermot made you his sole beneficiary."

"But a beneficiary of what?" She sagged into the high-backed leather chair as the full import of his meaning sunk in. "You just said the bank holds a mortgage on the property and that it's overdue."

"Actually it's quite a large mortgage. Your father recently renegotiated it."

"So how much do I owe on the place?"

Ephraim Thornbush enunciated the amount clearly and concisely, then folded his thin, long hands with their scrupulously clean and filed nails on top of the manila folder on his desk.

Dani could only stare at him while her mind tried to wrap itself around the latest in a series of unbelievable events. The only thing that brought order to this mess was when she focused on the man in front of her.

Mr. Thornbush's white hair lay in neat precise waves over his head. His black suit, perfectly tailored, showed no wrinkles, though it was past five o'clock on a Friday afternoon.

Dani glanced around the office. Not a speck of dust covered even one of the solid cherry surfaces. No half-empty coffee cup on his desk. Everything lay in its orderly arrangement, as it had for the past forty years.

Her father's lawyer abhorred untidiness in himself and his furnishings. He certainly wouldn't tolerate it in his legal practice. With Ephraim handling her father's estate, she knew every ''i'' was dotted, every ''t'' was crossed. There could be no mistake.

She gulped.

''I owe a fortune,'' she finally admitted, more to herself than to him. The massive amount of debt threatened to overwhelm her careful control. ''I had no idea he was in so much financial trouble. Why didn't he tell me?''

Mr. Thornbush did not say a word, but there was a gleam in his steel-gray gaze that made her shift uncomfortably.

''All right, I was out of touch over Christmas and New Year's. I admit that. But I called. He was never there.'' Dani fought to control the guilt that waited to swamp her. ''How could I know he was in the hospital?'' she whispered. ''How could I know he'd die?''

The steel softened to dove gray.

''There is no point in recriminations, Dani. What we must do now is make some decisions. I've delayed as much as possible while we located you. But the bank will not wait forever. They want assurances that they will get their money.''

''But I don't have any money.''

"I know." He picked up a pen, clicked it once, twice. Evidently he realized that the noise gave away his inner agitation, for he stopped fidgeting immediately and returned the pen to its holder.

"So what do I do now, Mr. Thornbush?" It hurt to ask that, stung her pride to know that she wasn't the strong independent woman she'd always thought herself. Coming back, especially now, only made her feel like a foolish girl who needed her daddy. And Daddy wasn't there. He never would be again.

"We could declare bankruptcy."

She jerked upward, her eyes narrowing.

"They'd take the land?"

He nodded. "Sell the cattle, your father's horses, machinery, anything that would bring in some money. The land would be auctioned off or they'd ask for bids. With the economy the way it is, I don't think they'd get top dollar."

"So not everyone would get their money back." She squinted at him. "You did say he owed more than the bank?"

"Your father had a few stocks, some bonds. He had me liquidate those just before he died. I paid off the local merchants. No one in Blessing will lose money because of your father, Dani. In fact, I doubt anyone even knows the seriousness of your situation."

"Thank goodness for that." At least she'd be spared the humiliation of having her hometown speculating about her any more than they already were.

Dani glanced at him. "Do you think that's what I should do?"

Mr. Thornbush did not answer immediately, which was, of itself, a most unusual thing, for he'd always been very quick to assess a situation. After all, he'd had two weeks since her father's death to think about it. She'd only learned of Dermot's passing on Monday, and about the ranch's fiscal nightmare just now.

"What is it? Is there something wrong?"

He shook his head. "Not wrong, exactly. It's simply that I believe your father wanted you to take over the ranch when you came home. Dermot didn't know when that would be, he certainly didn't expect that he wouldn't be here, but he often spoke of his intentions. I can't believe he would have wanted you to part with the land he loved so much, unless there was no other way."

"But there is no other way. Is there?"

"You could work it yourself. Cut back to the bare bones, run as tight a ship as you can while we try to find a way to appease the bank. Bankruptcy isn't in their best interest either, don't forget."

"Work it…myself?" She blinked. "But—"

"From the day he arrived in Blessing, Dermot was my friend. He loved that land all his life. I know he raised you to love it too. Don't you owe him and yourself a chance to see if you can make a go of it? You did say you weren't going back to college." He raised one bushy eyebrow, and when she didn't respond, he continued. "Why not spend some time out there, think things over, decide what your heart wants?"

It struck her as odd to hear Ephraim speaking about her heart's desire, but over the years Dani had occasionally caught glimpses of the lawyer's softer side. And he had cared deeply for Dermot.

"Maybe you're right. Everything's mixed up, confused. I'm a little shocked by his death—and now this. Maybe time will help me make a decision." She stood, thrust out her hand. "Thank you very much. If there's no rush to make an immediate decision, I think I'll do as you say and think it over."

"And pray about it. Don't forget to pray."

She smiled.

"Yes, I'll pray, too. Maybe God will send a miracle."

A wisp of a smile twitched the corner of his mouth.

"Someone once told me that God's miracles are that He uses time and circumstance to teach us more about Himself. Think of this as a learning curve, Dani. Steep, maybe, but we learn best when we're in the valley."

Dani shook his hand gratefully.

"I've been away a while," she told him. "But not long enough to forget Winifred Blessing. I'm sure she's your source for that advice."

Ephraim Thornbush only smiled. "Feel free to drop by whenever you wish. I'll help however I can."

"Thank you."

Dani walked through the office and outside to the brisk breeze of a February evening in Colorado. Winter still clung to the land, though a recent chinook had diminished its effects. Now darkness shrouded the little town in the foothills of the Rockies.

Blessing, Colorado. Home.

She strode over to her father's truck, climbed in and started the engine. Not many minutes later the heater blasted out gloriously warm air. But Dani's attention strayed to the church across the town square.

"This is our home, Dani. DeWitt roots are here, dug deep and strong into this soil. The Double D is our future. Yours and mine. Together we'll make it shine."

She'd been what, five? Old enough to snuggle into his arms and feel safe when a coyote yipped in the distance. She remembered how the sound had jarred her father from his contemplation of the land he loved, how he'd turned his horse toward home, holding her tightly in the circle of his arms.

Dermot was a fighter. He'd never given up on anyone or anything.

Neither would she. Not until she'd exhausted every last possibility.

Dermot DeWitt's name would not be smirched by bankruptcy.

Not if Dani could help it.

Chapter One

Wasn't home supposed to be the place you ran to when things got tough? So why did she want to run away from the only home she'd ever known?

"It just doesn't feel the same anymore, Duke."

Dani curled her fingers in the horse's thick black mane and surveyed the acres of ranch land that legally bore her name. The warm April winds had nudged the grass into a rich green, encouraged the wildflowers to bloom, melted the tufts of snow that tried to cling to the shadowed clefts of the hills. She could be a thousand miles away and picture this scene, and yet still it didn't feel right.

"The Double D isn't home. Not without Daddy."

Maybe it was the denim-striped overalls her father had wrapped up every year for Christmas, no matter how old she was. Maybe it was growing up on a ranch without a mother to curb her tomboy ways. Maybe it was because her best friend had always been a horse. Whatever the reason, most folks in Blessing had always accepted that Dani belonged on the Double D as much as syrup belonged on flapjacks.

Once, Dani would have agreed.

From her earliest years she'd ridden the perimeter of the ranch while chilly spring blazed into summer. She'd endured blizzard winters when going to town was impossible, and scorching summers when water became more precious than gold. She'd watched new colts wobble to their feet, spent hours waiting for the sun to turn bloodred before it slipped off the horizon. During all those years, Dani reveled in being in exactly the right place.

Until now.

Was it just because she'd been away at college for four years that she was only now realizing what a lonely life they'd led? Was that why Dermot had mortgaged his beloved land for her, so she'd know a different world than that of the Double D? Did it matter why? She was in hock up to her eyebrows and she had to get out.

"Stop whining, girl!" she ordered herself out loud. She didn't need anyone's shoulder to bawl on. She'd manage just fine on her own. Daddy would have expected that.

"We've got to stop thinking about what was, don't we, Duke."

Duke snorted as if to remind her that the past was hard to forget when the bank statements kept arriving.

"I have to put it out of my mind for tonight, though. There's that meeting at church about the dinner theater, and I'm in charge."

She'd agreed to help, believing that something other than the ranch and its debt baggage would be a relief to think about. Instead she'd encountered even more problems—when the director left town.

"Can I tell you a secret, Duke? I wish someone else would have volunteered to direct. I'm so tired of being in charge."

Reality check. There *was* no one else. Not for the Double D and apparently not for the dinner theater. The onus fell on her.

A whisper touch to his flanks sent Duke galloping across the tufted spring grass of her Colorado pasture as if chased by a pack of yapping dogs. Dani leaned over his neck and felt the wind whipping her hair as Duke galloped toward home—home for as long as she could hang onto it, at least.

At the barn she took her time brushing the big horse down, added a scoop of oats to his feed, ensured his water was topped up. For herself, a quick wash in hot, soapy water, a tug of the brush through her mop of black shiny curls and a change in jeans was enough. Funny how those jeans always made her feel taller, especially when she put her boots on. And goodness knows Dani could use a boost in height. She just hated being short, and no matter how tall your boots were, five foot three was short.

A routine check of the reflection in the mirror made her shrug. She'd do. Her lashes were thick enough to fringe her green eyes—"cat eyes," Daddy had called them. Not that she'd bothered with mascara since coming home. Life was too short and there were too many things to do on the ranch to fuss about makeup. Besides, her lipstick never stayed on longer than it took to smudge, and she'd never mastered the art of powder or foundation.

Dani stuck her tongue out at herself and giggled.

Who cared what she looked like anyway? She was alone most of the time. Tonight she simply had a job to do.

Her father's ancient half-ton truck sped her off the ranch and into Blessing Township efficiently enough that Dani decided to ignore its belch of protest when she shut off the engine.

"Don't even think about it, Red." She glared at one rusted fender. "The lead character's taken a hike, the cook's left for California, and I stupidly agreed to direct a play we're to put on in four months—with no lead actor. On top of everything else, I've got to figure out my next move with the ranch. I have no time to tinker with you."

"Excuse me?"

She whirled around, her eyes wide with shock. Nobody ever snuck up on Dani. Back in her school years, hard experience had taught teasing boys that she hated to be surprised. Maybe she'd lived down her reputation?

"Yes?"

Dani studied the handsome man before her, measured his sleepy brown eyes with their tiny fans of crinkles. He had the kind of smile you immediately trusted, which was exactly why she kept up her guard. Hadn't she learned the hard way that nothing was ever as it seemed? This lean man in his crisply pressed clothes sent a rush of energy through her bloodstream. Suddenly she wished she'd bothered with the mascara.

Just as quickly, Dani told herself to forget it. She had known a man as attractive as this one, and she'd been burned. It wouldn't happen again.

Who was he, anyway?

Dani thought she knew everyone in town, but she didn't know him. Did she? She took a second look at his uncombed mop of sandy hair and mentally shook her head. Nope. It was hardly likely she'd forget a man who looked as he did—loose-limbed, lanky, easygoing, as if he was comfortable in his skin and didn't care what anyone else thought. In fact, he was so relaxed, he made her feel uptight.

A flickering memory of a church potluck dinner given to welcome Blessing's newest doctor… It was right after Dr. Darling's accident. She'd been home for a weekend, she remembered. Dermot had wanted to leave church immediately to tend a sick calf, but everyone else had stayed. What was his name? Duke? she wondered, then nodded. Just like her horse.

"Can I help you, Dr. Duke?" she asked.

"Uh, actually it's Luc. Lucas Lawrence. But you did get the other part right. I am a doctor." He grinned, then his eyes widened. "Have you hurt yourself?"

"No." Why would he ask that? Dani followed his glance down, saw the jagged tear across her knee. Oh yeah. The rip. Well, mending was not her forte, even if she'd had time. "Thanks, but I'm fine. Just running a little late."

She turned, headed for the church. Behind her, his feet rattled on the pebbled surface. He was following her? Dani frowned, faced him.

"Maybe I can help you?" she offered, suspicion evident in her voice. She never used to be that way, but lately, well—

The doctor shook his head, grinned.

"I don't think so, but thanks anyway. I've been here long enough to know where the church is." He waited for her to move forward, and when she didn't, he walked around her, moved up the sidewalk and pulled open the church door. Half bending at the waist, he waved a hand as if to usher her inside. "After you, madam."

A decidedly English accent.

"Thanks." Dani stepped through the doorway, then stopped, her mind busy. Dr. Duke—no Luc—was perfect for the part. Tall, handsome—in a mussed sort of way. He spoke clearly, enunciated his words without drawling the vowels. "Say that again, please," she requested. "With the accent."

His eyes widened, but he obediently repeated the phrase.

"Excellent. You'll make a perfect Inspector Merrihew." She lowered her voice, leaned forward. "I'm pretty sure the part's yours, but please don't say anything. Not just yet, anyway."

"I beg your pardon? What part is mine?" Dr. Luc jerked to a halt, blinked at her, his brilliant smile faltering. His chocolate-brown eyes lost their sleepy look, darkened to a concerned brown-black; his body lost that slouchy appearance.

"Shh." She checked over each of her shoulders, then leaned toward him. "Inspector Merrihew. The tryouts are tonight. Isn't that why you're here?"

"Uh, no."

Dani frowned. Big Ed Warner wanted that part and wanted it badly. But Big Ed could in no way be made over into an English police inspector, not even if they pried away his ten-gallon hat, goaded his size fifteens from their hand-tooled cowboy boots, and raced him around town until he lost his paunch. Big Ed was a cowboy, plain and simple—a John Wayne wannabe.

"The thing is, I— Uh, that is, I was hoping I could help—"

"You *can* help. Accepting this part would be the big-

gest help, believe me.'' Dani took pity on his confusion.
''Go ahead and grab a seat in the fellowship hall, Doc.
I've got to get something from the pastor, then I'll be
there.''

''But— But—''

''Don't worry. You'll do fine.'' Dani tossed an encouraging smile over her shoulder, then strode toward
the office, hoping she was right about this new guy. A
doctor should be able to act. Didn't they have to hide
their emotions when they gave a patient bad news? This
Lucas Lawrence might just be the answer she'd prayed
for.

The pastor was out on a hospital call, but, as promised, he'd left the fax from the orphanage officials lying
on his desk. Dani's eyes widened at the dollar figure
scrawled across the bottom. *Total cost for renovations
needed before we can reopen. Tell Dani we'd love to
see her again. There's lots of work here.*

Dani brushed away the tear before it could drop. Two
short-term mission trips to Honduras after a terrible hur-
ricane devastated the area had left her appreciative of
everything she'd once taken for granted. She'd worked
hard to accomplish much in those one-month stints at
the orphanage. But now they needed more than a girl
with a hammer. They needed money to rebuild.

''Money they'll receive—if we can just get this show
off the ground.''

She squeezed her eyes closed and whispered another
prayer for help. First the ranch and Daddy—now this.
Was all the world hurting?

Gathering her courage, Dani returned to the sanctuary. God would help, just as He was helping her work
out things on the ranch. It didn't mean there wouldn't
be more questions. It simply meant she had to look to

Him for the answers. She'd just have to keep plod-
ding away.

Back in the hall, Dani noticed Dr. Lucas Lawrence
had chosen a spot four pews from the back. He sat
hunched over, staring at the confusion up front. As if
he knew she was there, he turned, met her gaze, raised
one eyebrow, then returned his attention to the platform,
forehead pleated in a frown.

People milled about, chattering in small groups. They
were willing enough to help, Dani knew, just unsure of
where to begin. They needed a goal. With barely four
months left until opening night, nothing had been decided. Somebody had to step in, and thanks to Pastor
Bob, Miss Winifred Blessing and Dani's own big
mouth, Dani had been elected as director.

She took a deep breath and walked down the aisle.

"Okay, folks. If we can all be seated up here, I'd like
to get started." She smiled as Miss Blessing hushed the
two most vocal of her helpers. The staple of Blessing
Township, Miss Winifred was a godsend Dani was con-
tinually thankful for. If anyone could help her get
through this, Miss Winifred could.

"First off, I'd like to know if there is anyone who
would like the director's job. Anyone at all?" Dead
silence filled the auditorium. "I was afraid of that,"
Dani muttered.

"Come on, Dani. You can do it." Encouraging
voices cheered their support.

There was no way out. Did she really want one?
Wasn't this the opportunity she'd prayed for—a chance
to stage one of her own plays? Dani remembered advice
she'd once been given in Miss Winifred's Sunday
school class. *Be careful what you pray for. You might
get it.*

"All right, people, you asked for it. But everybody's going to have to pitch in." They nodded their agreement. "Great. Tonight I'd like us to strike the committees and get some solid work done."

"About time we got going." Murmurs of agreement echoed around the room.

"This is the list I've been given. To begin with—Emmy, we need to get some sketches under way for the publicity fliers and handouts. Pastor Bob said you'd offered?"

From the corner of her eye, Dani saw the new doctor move forward, seating himself at the back of the group. He didn't speak to anyone, merely nodded at a few people who smiled at him.

Emmy described her ideas.

"Excellent. I knew that marketing degree of yours was going to come in handy," Dani teased. "If you can get some advertising ideas worked up in the next couple of days, I'd love to see them. Now, we need hosts and hostesses for the actual evening. Volunteers?" As soon as one vacancy was filled, Dani moved on to the next. There was so much to do.

"Big Ed, I'm counting on you for the backdrops. Nobody can build like you." The tall man blushed his pleasure. Dani smiled at him. "I mean it. If ever there was a gift given for building stuff, you've got it. We all know that if you put it together, it's going to stand. No doubts there. How soon can you get the sets organized? Don't forget Anita has to paint them."

"I was kinda counting on—" He stumbled to a halt, his face red.

Dani rushed to help him out. "A drawing. Right. I forgot. Sorry." The details just kept coming. Dani glanced out over the audience. "Will someone volunteer to sketch the backdrops so Big Ed will know what we need? I can give you the information, what there is of it, but when it comes to artwork I'm a washout." She saw a thin white arm move just the slightest, and grinned at her next-door neighbor. "Aha! Marissa McGonigle, don't you dare pull your hand back down. You can whip up those sketches without too much fuss, can't you?"

Marissa glanced at her husband, Gray, noted his shrug, and nodded. Her eyes flashed with excitement. "I'll do it, Dani. I'd love to have a part of this."

"Bless you. You see, folks, I knew she'd volunteer if I helped her."

Everyone chuckled. They were probably glad someone would be taking responsibility, Dani decided. As if she needed more responsibility. She pushed aside the doubts and concentrated on the next job the pastor had assigned.

"'Table setting and decorations,'" she read off the neatly typed list, aware that the new doctor was now beginning to fidget. *Please don't let him leave yet.*

"The wife and I've got that one under control, Danielle. Sure could use some helpers, though." Barry Quiggle's voice carried clearly.

"You'll get them." Would the new doctor back out? Her nerves stretched taut. So many people were depending on her. She couldn't let them down. She wouldn't. "Okay, we're making good progress. We'll get down to actually practicing in a second, just bear with me. Next on the list is the meal. As you all know, Maddie took off on us to get married. Hardly a good excuse!"

Muted laughter.

"Any volunteers?" Dani looked around hopefully.

But knowing the amount of work involved in feeding a crowd of two hundred, she didn't have the faintest hope that anyone would volunteer to coordinate this aspect. "Come on, you guys. If it's a dinner theater, we have to have dinner. Let's consider this together. We can't give up now."

After a long and painful silence, Dani was startled to see the doctor shuffle to his feet.

"I'm new here and I suspect you'll tell me to mind my own business." He stopped, pretended to ignore the few teasing catcalls, a forced smile on his lips. His long fingers gripped the pew in front so tight, his muscles bunched.

Why was he so nervous?

"Everybody gets a chance to make suggestions on this project." Dani held up her hand to quiet the whispering between two of the town's worst gossips. "Let's hear what he has to say. Go ahead, Dr. Luc. What are you thinking?"

"It's just that, um, I heard that Miss Winifred Blessing leads the women's auxiliary at the church. Well, you know—I presume they've fed a lot of people over the years, and no one's gone hungry." Nods of agreement seemed to embolden him. "I was wondering if she might give us some idea of what will be involved in a dinner of this magnitude."

All eyes turned on the town's gray-haired baker, who stood to her white-sneakered feet, a rose blush tinting her parchment cheeks.

"Luc, that's very dear of you to say." She smiled at the doctor. "I suppose I have had experience. As a matter of fact, I have made some notes. Just a few squiggles about quantities and such." She smiled at everyone.

"When you get to be my age, you make lists on everything, you know. Before you forget."

Appreciative laughter.

"So if recruits were found to handle the various tasks in the kitchen, would you be willing to head up the dinner committee, Miss Blessing?" Luc asked.

Dani stared at the doctor, amazed by his temerity. She wouldn't have dared ask such a thing, but it was as if Luc knew something the rest of them didn't. How could that be? He was the newcomer in town!

"If no one minds a bossy old woman fussing at them, I'd be delighted to lend my assistance to this worthy cause." Miss Blessing smiled happily, apple cheeks glowing. "Working together, I think we can manage quite well. Besides, Dani's agreed to handle so much, I think this is one area she should be free of."

"You wouldn't be volunteering because you've tasted Dani's cooking, would you, Miss Blessing?"

The room erupted in laughter at Big Ed's knowing wink. Dani grinned, not embarrassed in the least.

"Come on, Big Ed. I burned those cookies years ago. I've been to college since then, you know."

"Yeah, I heard." He nodded, his Stetson tilted back on his head. "Didn't think you were studying cooking, though. Dermot said it was some highfalutin stuff you read in books. And I don't mean recipe books."

The mention of her father's name sent a ping straight to her heart, but Dani refused to allow her smile to slip. It had been over three months since his death. When would the pain ease?

She'd learned a lot of things from her father, but one thing she'd never forget. *"Personal problems are just that—personal. We don't spill our guts to the neighbors, Dani."*

"Aw, give Dani a break," someone called. "Doesn't matter if she can't cook, as long as she can get this play going. We've got our caterer, and nobody could do it better than Miss Winifred."

"Well, if you're sure…" Miss Winifred waited for dissent, then nodded briskly. "All right, I'll do it."

The entire group heaved a collective sigh of relief. No one wanted to tackle a meal of such magnitude, but their busy little baker was exactly the right person to bring order out of chaos.

"It seems the meal is taken care of. Miss Winifred, I thank you for offering and we all pledge to do whatever you need. You just let us know how we can help." Dani glanced around the group, noticed everyone nodding.

"I'll do my best." Miss Winifred sat down, her face wreathed in smiles.

"Well, that's most of my list. Thank you, all." Dani scribbled a note to herself, then looked up. "I think we're about ready to rehearse. As soon as we audition for the main character, that is. We won't need all of you here for that." She glanced down at her list, then around. "Could I ask that the various committees please use the Sunday school rooms for your meetings? We need to conduct a read-through out here, so I'm asking for a bit of quiet."

Amid much chatter, the group broke up. Dani bent to pick up her copy of the play and noticed Dr. Luc inching his way up the aisle. They still needed a main character, and the pastor had insisted that it was up to her to find one. Dr. Luc was perfect. She couldn't let him get away— But Miss Winifred stopped her from following him.

"I do hope I won't disappoint, Dani dear," the baker murmured. "It is such a large job."

"I know you'll do fine." Dani stood on her tiptoes, saw Luc in the foyer. "Miss Winifred, I need another favor." She explained her difficulty. "He's the only one who suits the part." She dropped her voice to a whisper. "I just can't see Big Ed as an English inspector. Can you?"

"It does rather boggle the mind, doesn't it." Miss Blessing wrapped her fingers around Dani's. "Come along, dear. Time for a little teamwork. Lucas!" Her voice warbled through the sanctuary, carrying like a wind chime in the forest. "Luc, dear. Dani and I must speak with you. Coffee break, actors. Rehearsal in five."

They caught him entering the young-adult Sunday-school classroom which had been newly designated for use by the set-building committee.

"Luc, we need to talk to you."

"Oh." A wary glance passed over them. "I was just about to get in on this meeting for building props. I thought I might help them out."

"You?" Gray McGonigle stood beside Dani, his eyes huge with disbelief. "What did you ever build?"

"Nothing." The doctor's face darkened in a red flush. "But I can learn."

"Indeed you can, dear. But not tonight. Tonight we need you to think about a higher mission." Miss Winifred wrapped one arm through Luc's and drew him next door, into the nursery. She closed the door as soon as Dani was through. "Much higher, my boy."

"Uh, I see."

He clearly didn't. Dani almost giggled at the panicked look crossing the good doctor's face.

"The inspector," she reminded him. "Remember? We need someone to play the inspector."

"But—" He glanced right and left, as if searching for help. "I don't think I'm your man. I've never done any acting. I just wanted to build something, maybe get to know people."

"Oh, you'll meet lots of people. Plus you'll help us raise funds for an orphanage in Honduras. It's really not that difficult a part, Luc dear. You just have to get the timing right." Miss Winifred patted his shoulder helpfully.

"No." He shook his head, his eyes moving from Dani to Miss Blessing and back again in frantic appeal. "No. I can't do it. I'm sure there must be someone else."

"But—"

He shook his head, his brown eyes glittering like dark ice as they settled on Dani. "I can't. That's all there is to it. I'm sure there's someone else you can call on."

Now what? Dani didn't know what to say.

"You're right, Luc." Winifred drooped, her sigh heartfelt. "It's too much to ask of a newcomer to town."

"But—"

Dani frowned, half glared at the older woman. To her surprise, Miss Winifred turned her head and winked. Her voice continued in a sad, almost whining tone.

"Why, think of how long it will take to memorize the lines, to come to practice, to find a costume. And you're such a busy doctor." She clicked her teeth together, paused a moment, then continued, as if a new thought had just hit. Her twinkling eyes met Dani's for a fraction of a second, but that was long enough for Dani to glimpse the mischief glittering there.

"I don't know what in the world I was thinking of, to volunteer for KP, either. Mercy, girl, I own a business, I'm on more committees than I can name, and I have my great-nephew's daughters to watch out for. There's no way on earth I can manage the kitchen for this play. No way at all."

Lucas frowned at her. "But you have to. There isn't anyone else who can do it."

"Someone will step into the gap," the baker assured him blithely. "If they don't, well then, we'll know God has other plans."

Winifred's blue eyes brightened. Dani lifted a hand to smother her giggle, risked a quick look at the doctor.

"But—but that's ridiculous!" He shook his head. "God can't accomplish things if people aren't willing to help."

"Exactly." Winifred Blessing's face glowed with satisfaction. "I'll be willing to help in the kitchen as long as you're willing to be the inspector Dani needs. Or are you going to wimp out on us?"

"Wimp—" The doctor straightened as if someone had refused to allow him to treat a patient. "I am not *wimping* out!"

"Of course you are, dear. And if you can do it, I can do it. After all, I'm older, with years of age-wearing troubles to deal with. Managing a meal this size will tire me for days. I've got a weak heart, too."

"Hah. There's nothing wrong with your heart. I did your physical last week, remember?" Luc cast Dani a dubious glance, then peered more closely into Miss Blessing's bland countenance. "This is a con."

"Is it?" Dani shrugged. "Miss Blessing has never said a thing she didn't mean in all the years I've known her. I don't think she's about to start now."

"But you've already got someone. I heard on coffee row that Big Ed said he was going to read for the part." He dared them to refute it.

"He's offered." Dani nodded. "He *could* memorize the lines, play the part."

"But?" Luc frowned at them both, chocolate-brown eyes wary. "There is a but, isn't there."

"Big Ed is a cowboy. He's a wonderful man, but we could never make him into an English inspector. We need someone younger, better suited to the part. We want the whole project to succeed beyond expectations. We want to see enough funding come in to rebuild that orphanage. Do you honestly think Big Ed can do that?" Dani fell silent, unable to communicate how deeply this need touched her, how certain she was that the doctor was the man for the part.

"There's a passage in the Bible," Miss Winifred murmured. "I forget the exact words, and I'll have to look up the reference, but the gist of it is that we should strive to do the best we can for God, not offer Him the mediocre."

"But you don't even know if I can do this," Luc challenged, glaring at them.

"I don't know if I can direct, either," Dani reminded him. "But I'm willing to step into the gap rather than see the whole project go under. Let's sink or swim together, shall we, Dr. Duke?" She said it deliberately, hoping to rouse some emotion in the reticent doctor.

"Luc," he corrected her in a loud voice. "It's Luc." He sighed. "If I won't try out, you won't help with the meal?" He waited for Miss Blessing's nod.

Her grin made Winifred look far younger than her age, which, in fact, remained a well-kept secret in Blessing Township.

"That about sums it up, Lucas."

"So, if I don't step in, everyone will blame me for the failure of the dinner theater." He sighed. "That's blackmail, you know."

"It is, isn't it?" Miss Winifred shrugged. "Oh well. Whatever works. When you get to be my age, you'll have learned that. Among other things."

Dani waited, holding her breath. Finally Luc tossed up his hands in defeat.

"I'll read for it," he said. "But you have to promise that if Big Ed is better, you'll give him the part. No more shenanigans."

"Agreed."

He pulled open the door, waited till they'd walked through.

"I just wanted to nail a few boards," Dani heard him mumble almost beneath his breath. "Saw something, maybe. Just a little construction work."

"Well, maybe we can arrange—" Gray McGonigle's hand on her arm stopped Dani midsentence. "Oh, hi, Gray. Did you want to talk to me?"

"Yes. Now. Please."

Dani stepped aside to let the others pass, stared at him in confusion.

"What's wrong?" she asked, half-afraid to hear the answer.

"Dani, I'm not trying to run the show or anything, believe me. I only want the best for this dinner theater, just as you do. So trust me when I ask you to keep Dr. Lucas Lawrence away from any and all construction. No saws, no nails, no hammers." He winced. "Particularly no hammers."

Dani frowned at the intensity underlying his words. "May I ask you why?"

"You know that house we rent out?"

She nodded.

"Last week Luc moved in. The other day he decided to hang a picture."

Dani shrugged, impatient to get on with the job. "So what?"

"Three hundred and forty-two dollars and seventy-eight cents, so far. That's what."

"Three hundred—" She stared. "How?"

"Looking for a stud, he said." Gray shuddered. "Made a hole in the drywall, knocked over a floor lamp, which tipped and went through the picture window."

The giggle just would not be denied. Dani slapped a hand over her mouth to muffle it. "Oh dear."

"Easy for you to say. I was fool enough to accept his offer to help me fix things." He held up one hand with a thick bandage around his thumb. "Luc Lawrence is a great doctor and I like him very much, but he couldn't hit the broad side of a barn door with a sledge-hammer. I sure don't want him touching anything in here." His eyes rested on the beautiful oak panels the deacons had just ordered installed at the front of the church. "Know what I mean?"

"Yes, I do. Leave it to me, Gray. I'll think of something." Dani giggled again before patting his arm. "Poor thing. Maybe you should ask Marissa to kiss your boo-boo better. That seems to work well for your son."

Ignoring his pained look, she turned and walked back into the hall, aware that Gray followed just a few steps behind. She couldn't look at him for fear she'd start laughing, so she focused on the doctor. He looked worried. Why was that?

"All right, everyone, let's start reading."

The actors scrambled to find their copies and get into character. Everyone except Lucas Lawrence. He stood where he was and glared at her. Miss Winifred perched on the first chair in the first row, arms crossed over her chest, lips pursed. Dani took a deep breath and walked forward.

"What's the matter now?" she asked, keeping her voice soft so the others wouldn't hear.

"Luc is being obstreperous."

"I am not." He tipped back on his heels, his face rigidly composed. "We'd be wise to look at all the angles. I have a valid concern."

Dani looked to Winifred, found no help there. She sighed. "Which is?"

"I'm a temporary doctor in this town. What if I leave before the dinner theater is held?"

She frowned. He was too calm. Dani squinted, assessing him. Her daddy would have said the man squirmed just a bit too much.

"Are you planning on leaving Blessing soon, Doc?" she asked.

"No, he's not." Winifred shook her head.

"How do you know what I'm planning?"

"I just do."

Luc frowned at her. "Well, you don't know about this."

"You're not going anywhere." Miss Blessing swung her foot back and forth, her mouth tipped into a triumphant smile as she winked at Dani. "Otherwise, why did he invite his sister to visit him here at Christmas?"

"Of all the nerve—" He cut off his tirade, fumed silently.

Miss Blessing smiled innocently. "I didn't deliberately listen in on your conversation, Lucas, but you were standing in my bakery when you said it.''

Defeat dragged his shoulders down. Dani suddenly felt a pang of sympathy for him. They had bulldozed over his objections. Still, he would be good, she just knew it. All he had to do was try.

"Give it a shot," she encouraged. "Just one read-through. Please?"

"You don't understand." He turned his back on Miss Blessing, dropped his voice to a whisper. "I can't."

"Why not?"

"Stage fright. I stand up in front of a crowd and my mind goes totally blank." He shook his head, his thin cheeks flushed. "Speeches, stories, poems—doesn't matter how well I know them, I simply can't repeat them in front of a bunch of people. My jaw locks up, my heart starts thudding and I can't get a word out. I've struggled with it for years. As an actor, I'm the bottom of the barrel. Choose someone else. Please?"

"There is no one else, Luc. Just you. Please don't give up." Dani offered a smile to bolster his courage, certain it must have been hard for him, a competent doctor, to admit this flaw. "I'll help. I'm a pretty good director." *I think.*

"You'll need to be." Seeing the expectant faces around him, Luc sighed, then nodded. "Oh, all right. Just don't say I didn't warn you," he whispered.

"I won't."

He lifted his lips in a sickly smile and followed her directions, moving to a seat in the front row. He picked up a copy of the play and read his part. As one of many among the cast, he seemed to lose his nervousness, his confidence growing as he continued through to the end of the play. Dani wondered if he'd been teasing about the stage fright.

"This is very good. Who wrote it?" He turned the sheets over, searching for the author.

Dani smiled, but ignored the question. "I'm glad you like it. I think you'll make a great inspector."

Her decision was echoed by the other players, spirits rejuvenated now that someone had finally been found who could read the lines with impact.

"If no one objects, I suggest the part of Inspector Merrihew be assigned to Dr. Luc. What do you think?"

Heads nodded in agreement all around the room.

Big Ed's beefy fist shot up as he began to speak, his excitement obvious. "The boy's perfect for that part. No denying that. Has that accent down pat. I never could get the hang of that."

Dani nodded, delighted with the cowboy's easy acceptance of Luc.

"Great. It's unanimous. Now, Inspector, do you want to try the part on stage?"

"I—I guess."

But he didn't, she could see that in the hunted look in his eyes. *Try,* she begged silently. *Just try.*

"'Gertrude Mortimer baked the best chocolate cake anyone had ever tasted.' Now you say it."

He stood at center stage, stared at her. Dani repeated the phrase.

"Gertrude Chocolate mortimered anyone..." He stopped, gulped.

The others chuckled in sympathy.

"You'll get it. Just keep trying," the crowd encouraged.

But Luc didn't get it. Half an hour later Dani dismissed the rest of the cast and watched them scurry away, undoubtedly grateful they didn't have to endure any more of his line-mangling.

"It was distracting with the others here," she excused as the door banged shut for the tenth time. "Way too noisy. We'll practice one-on-one. Don't worry about it. Come on, let's try it down here."

"You can't say I didn't warn you." He sighed, took the stairs two at a time and flopped down beside her. This time the words emerged perfectly. But as soon as they returned to the stage to practice their movements with the lines, he tightened up, forgot what he was doing.

By ten-thirty Dani was ready to phone Big Ed and beg him to take over. Unfortunately Winifred Blessing didn't know the meaning of the word *defeat.*

"Tiredness, that's all it is. Simply too weary. Everyone's had a long, busy day. So many things to do." She cluck-clucked her sympathy, patting Luc's shoulder as if he were four. "Try again when you're fresh, dear. You too, Dani."

Dani hadn't felt fresh since the day she'd found out her father had left the ranch submerged in debt. But she scrounged for a bit of cheerfulness.

"This is Thursday," she murmured, trying to remember what she'd planned for the weekend. "I've got some stuff to do Saturday morning, but maybe you could come out to the ranch in the afternoon. Around one? I could coach you then."

"Why prolong the inevitable? I'm lousy at this." Luc shrugged at her glower. "Oh, all right, fine. Saturday afternoon. I'll be there, barring a medical emergency. But this is a waste of time. I'm not an actor, I'm a doctor. And no matter how badly you want to, you can't change me.''

Thus released, he walked quickly up the aisle and left the building.

Dani waited until she heard the outer door squeak closed. Then she turned to Miss Winifred.

"Are you sure—"

Winifred patted her shoulder, her face beaming. "The Lord works in mysterious ways, Dani. But He does perform His wonders. Just you give Him a chance."

Which was all well and fine, Dani decided as she pulled into her yard half an hour later. But they had only four months, and Dr. Lucas Lawrence hadn't memorized three paragraphs in three hours. She climbed out, reached in for her jacket and blinked. A little white bakery box with that familiar red script was nestled on her back seat.

"'Blessing Bakery,'" she read aloud, stomach rumbling at the thought of delicacies she'd often seen tucked inside boxes like these. "'Made with love.'" She lifted the lid to peek inside. "What have you done now, Miss Winifred?"

One of Miss Blessing's heart-shaped love cookies lay inside. The cookies were famous, appearing in unexpected spots all over the county, but Dani had never before received one personally. She held the box under the truck's interior light, curious about the message she knew would be piped across the cookie in vivid red icing.

Faith isn't faith until it's all you're holding on to.

As usual, Miss Winifred's cookie stated the problem with a piercing succinctness that made Dani wince.

"I'm trying to have faith, Lord," she whispered, lifting the cookie out and nibbling off one corner as she stared at the blanket of stars winking overhead. "But tonight didn't help. Ranch problems are bad enough. What am I going to do with an actor who freezes up the minute he gets on stage?"

The night breeze swirled off the snow-capped mountains and down around her, a chilling reminder that winter might not be finished yet. Loath to leave this panorama of beauty before her for the silence of her empty home, Dani remained a moment longer, considered nights past when she'd felt as if she nestled in the Father's hand.

Heaven's kiss, her dad had called it. A feeling that God leaned down and brushed your cheek with His lips, that He was in charge and everything would be fine. It had been so long since she'd felt that tender care.

"Everyone's gone home to their families. Dad's with You. But I'm out here all alone, God." The words, whispered on the night air, carried back to her in painful repetition.

Alone. Alone. Alone.

Dani waited for that featherlight caress of peace to flow through her weary heart. But only the nip of frosty air brushed over her cheeks.

Evidently heaven wasn't in a kissing mood tonight.

Chapter Two

On Saturday, just after lunch, Dr. Lucas Lawrence steered his car around an assortment of potholes that littered the road to the Double D ranch and wondered why anyone willingly chose to live out here.

Just as quickly he chided himself for the criticism.

"Okay, it's beautiful," he admitted, gazing at the quilt-block pattern that the variegated greens made across the landscape. "Creation in all its glory." He winced at the bounce from the right front wheel. "But it's miles from civilization and a death trap to drive over!"

A sudden thought made him chuckle.

"If Winifred Blessing were here, she'd call me a wimp." He deliberately pressed down the accelerator. One bone-jarring thump later, he yelped and immediately lifted his foot.

"I probably am a wimp." He admitted it with a sigh and eased his aching behind more firmly into the padded seat, his attention fixed on the road.

"Now what?" Just on the crest of the next hill, a

lone cow stood in the middle of the road, back end facing him. There wasn't enough room on either side to pass the beast. Luc honked the horn.

The placid cow turned to face him. To his dismay, the cow turned out to be a bull that apparently was not amused by honking car horns. It scraped one hoof against the ground and snorted its protest in a bellow of disgust.

"Carrying bucolic a bit far, aren't we, God?"

He sat there for several moments, waiting for inspiration to strike. The bull glared at him. Luc glared back. He was no wimp. He was a tough, in-charge doctor. He twisted the steering wheel hard right and edged forward. The bull moved just slightly to the right. Luc shifted to the left, so did the bull.

He considered getting out and chasing the thing away, but he'd chosen his favorite red shirt to wear today, and some echo in his memory reminded him that bulls charged anything red.

"What exactly am I doing out here?" he muttered in disgust. "Saturday afternoon and I'm sitting here trading stares with a bull." As weekend entertainment, Luc felt it lacked a certain something.

The roar of an engine struggling to climb a hill caught his attention. Moments later Dani DeWitt's battered red truck drew up beside the bull. Luc switched off his engine, his attention snagged by her chiding voice.

"Marvin, what are you doing out here?" She grabbed one horn and pulled. The beast shook his head free, then leaned over to lick her face.

"Stop that!" She dragged a shirtsleeve across her face. "I'm not impressed with your affections, you know. You're supposed to be in the south paddock, not out here blocking traffic."

The beast snuffled a response, rubbing its massive head against her side in a way that made Luc reach for the door handle as fear snaked its way up his spine. She couldn't weigh one-tenth as much as that mammoth. It would surely kill her. He pushed the door open, freezing when it creaked loudly. The bull turned to glare at him.

Dani DeWitt didn't even glance his way.

"Don't get out, Doc. Just stay where you are. I have everything under control."

Sure she did.

Luc didn't believe it for a moment, but presumably she did have more knowledge than he about this animal. She even knew the thing's name, though he'd never have called something so impossibly ugly "Marvin."

Luc patted the seat beside him. He had his cell phone. He could call for help if he needed it, though he wasn't clear on exactly whom to call.

"Okay, Marv. Shift your bulk right now, and I mean it. I've got my zapper and if you give me a bit of trouble, I'll poke you right in the rump."

The bull nudged her thigh again, waggled its horns, then obediently plodded across the road, into the ditch, and daintily stepped over a broken strand of electric fence. Dani followed him and smacked him on the hind quarters.

"You get home right now, Marvin, or you'll find yourself going without supper tonight. Git now!" She stood her ground, hands on her hips, glaring at the beast's wavering back end.

Marvin emitted a strange bellow, nodded his giant head twice, then began to trot due north, his hooves thundering against the hard-packed ground.

Luc climbed out of his car, staring at her in astonishment.

"How did you do that?"

"Hey, Doc. Didn't think you were coming." Dani touched her cheek with one finger, grimaced and wiped her face on her shirttail. She made a face at the wet spot of bull saliva, then grinned at him. "That dumb ol' bull thinks I'm his daughter."

"His daughter?" He chuckled. "You scared the daylights out of me when you grabbed his horn."

"Oh, Marvin won't hurt me. We grew up together. But don't ever put yourself between him and me. He's very protective. My dad once yelled at me and Marvin charged him." She giggled. "He's really just a big old softie, but he doesn't like everyone to know that. Especially men."

"I see." Luc swallowed. This—this girl had used a few choice words to single-handedly manage what he'd seen grown men twice her size fail at. His appreciation for Dani DeWitt's courage soared. "I'm sorry I'm so late. M-Marvin wouldn't let me past."

"No, he doesn't want any strangers on the ranch. He's afraid I'll sell him like I did the other cattle." Her face changed, lost its glow of fun.

"Will you?" He saw how little she wanted that to happen.

"Probably have to," she murmured. "I don't have any cows to breed him with and he's worth a fair bit."

"I'm sorry." He didn't know what else to say.

"Thanks. It's been tough since Dad died, but I'm getting through."

"From all I've heard, you're doing very well."

Her head jerked up at that, eyes narrowed. Luc realized he'd just told her the entire town was talking about her. He hurried to change the subject.

"Is this your land?"

She nodded. "Far as you can see."

She told him exactly how many acres she owned, but the number didn't compute in his brain.

"It sounds big, but I know less than nothing about ranches."

"Why would you? You're a doctor. I know less than nothing about medicine." She pointed down the road. "If you want to follow me, I'll take you back to the house."

"Weren't you headed somewhere? I don't want to take up your afternoon." Maybe he could get out of this yet.

"I was expecting you. I just came out to check on Marvin. I knew he'd head out here. He does it whenever he wants to make a statement." She turned toward her truck. "Keep driving straight ahead. You'll see the house in about five miles."

Luc followed her at some distance, hoping to avoid the cloud of dust that trailed behind her truck, but also wanting to save wear on his shocks. Pavement appeared to be in short supply in Dani DeWitt's neck of the woods.

As he drove, Luc noted that the place was huge—miles of green stretched before him. She ran it virtually alone, he knew from gossip in town. He couldn't help his smile of admiration. Dani DeWitt was one very unusual woman. She'd handled a bull with an attitude, agreed to direct a play that involved half the town. She was feisty. And she sure didn't back down from a challenge. He'd experienced that personally.

The house, when he saw it, made his eyes widen. A

large, cedar-sided two-storey, it sat in the lee of a south-facing hill, huge windows offering what must be a stunning vista over the surrounding valley. A few scraggly flowers struggled to show their blooms against the house, but mostly the yard was grass. He parked beside her truck, climbed out.

"It's very beautiful country," he told her sincerely. "You must love to come home."

"Yes, I do. I was away at college for four years, but every time I came back, it was as if I'd never left." She motioned to the willow furniture on the deck outside the front door. "Would you like to sit out here in the sun? I can get us some lemonade."

"Sure." Luc gingerly lowered himself onto the cushion atop a web of woven willow and found it quite comfy. He waited, content to study the magnificent view, until she returned with two frosty glasses. "Thanks."

"You're welcome." She took a sip, stared at him for a moment. "Are you enjoying Blessing, Dr. Lawrence?"

"It's Luc." He nodded. "Yes, I am. Now that Joshua's recovered and I have a few minutes of spare time, I'm looking forward to really getting to know the area."

"It was a terrible accident. I know both he and Nicole were glad you were there." Dani stared out across the billowing grasses. "They seem very happy together."

"I'm sure they are. The girls love their new mother, and Nicole doesn't let Joshua get away with much. She's got her own opinions about things." He didn't want to talk about work, Luc discovered. He wanted to talk about her. He didn't bother to ask himself why. "Tell me about the ranch."

A mask fell over her eyes, shielding her thoughts from him.

"What do you want to know?"

He shrugged. "Whatever you want to tell me. What it's like to live out here. Whether you intend on staying or not."

"Staying? Of course I'm staying. Who told you otherwise?" Her brows drew together in a frown of dismay.

"No one's said anything. I just assumed with you being so young, you'd rather move back to the city." He glanced around, noted the unmown grass, the windows that needed painting, the broken board in the balustrade. "You must get lonely out here by yourself."

"I don't really." She smiled. "Maybe because I'm so busy, or maybe it's because I grew up here, cut my teeth on a horse's bridle. This is my world."

"And you love it."

It didn't take the nod of her head to tell him that. Luc could see it in the way she stroked the arm of her chair, in the softness of her eyes as she watched horses frolic in a distant pasture. Dani possessed a beauty he'd seldom seen. She had a youthful vitality that glowed in her vivid green eyes, glittered in the sheen of her black hair where the sun struck, but it was more than that.

Her beauty stemmed from the easy way she fit into her world, accepted its problems and refused to moan about it. He'd heard enough talk to know she'd inherited trouble.

"Yes, I do love the Double D. I just hope I can hang onto it."

Luc wasn't sure how to answer that. He'd got the impression she was sensitive about gossip, but he also had a hunch she needed someone to talk to. Listening was something his profession had made him fairly good at, and Dani DeWitt's low melodic voice was easy to listen to.

"I'm sure it's a lot of work for one person."

She glanced at him, then shifted her eyes away. "I have— I had help. I had to let most of them go. Now I share a hand with Gray McGonigle. He does most of the heavy work, so it's not too bad."

Luc glanced down at her fingers, saw the calluses that covered her small palms and felt a pang of sympathy for the chores she'd undertaken. She was so young to be saddled with such a demanding task.

"I'll soon have to get rid of the rest of the stock," she murmured, her eyes on a herd grazing a quarter of a mile away.

He understood she was thinking out loud, so Luc leaned back in his chair and sipped his lemonade.

"They're too much for me to handle and I can't afford to feed them come winter. Besides, I need the money they'll bring." Her voice dropped until it emerged a faint whisper. "I wish he'd told me about the loan. I didn't have to go to college. I would have been quite happy to stay right here." She peered up at Luc, her eyes glassy with tears.

"I'm sure your father wanted his daughter to experience college life, Dani. I didn't know him well, but I don't think he would have begrudged you the opportunity, no matter what it cost. Let me tell you something I've learned, just from watching Joshua Darling. Nothing is too much for a man's daughters." He kept his eyes straight ahead, pretended he wasn't paying attention to her soft sniffles as she struggled for control.

"Daddy insisted I go. At first we even argued about it. But I never could disobey him. Still, I should have refused. I didn't realize he was so short of cash. He shouldn't have taken out a loan to send me on that over-seas study trip last summer. He should have told me. I'd have come home sooner if I'd known.''

''If you'd known he didn't have long to live, you mean?'' Luc did look at her then, touched by her sense of loss. ''Dani, your father wouldn't have wanted you to put your life on hold, waiting for him to die. He was happy living each day. He put the most he could into his time here, and then his heart failed him. Some men suffer for years, but he didn't. Be glad you had the time you did.''

''I am.'' She sighed. ''It's just…hard. You know? I didn't even get to say goodbye.''

''I know.'' He met her tear-filled eyes. ''I was there, I heard him talking about you. He loved you very much.'' Who was he to give advice? Still Luc searched for encouragement. ''Try to remember the good times you shared. And if you need a friend, I'll be here.''

''Thanks. I might take you up on that.'' She nodded, took a swipe at her tears. ''Do you have a family?''

''One sister, two brothers.'' He remembered suddenly that he hadn't written any of them in ages. E-mail wasn't that difficult to send. He chided himself for not keeping better touch.

''That must have been fun.'' A wistful longing filled her voice. ''I would have loved a sister.''

''Not mine, you wouldn't. She was a pain.'' Tracy's stubbornness had not abated in the years since her pre-school temper tantrums, though Luc had never told her that outright. He preferred a hassle-free existence.

''Did you argue?'' Dani's face lit up with interest, green eyes sparkling.

''All the time. She always knew what was right and,

unless you did it her way, she nagged you like a festering boil.''

"Doc!" Dani's laughter bubbled out in spite of her shocked look. "That's not very flattering.''

"Tracy's not the kind of sister you flatter. I'm just glad I was never a patient under her care.'' He made a face. "You'd get well just so you could escape.''

"She's a doctor or a nurse?''

"A bossy, cantankerous nurse who always knows what's best for everyone. Believe me, it wasn't any hardship to give her away when she got married.'' He strove for a lighthearted tone, hoping to ease her sad memories—while hoping Tracy would forgive him for enhancing his characterization of her managerial ways.

"Stubborn? Oh, she's like you, then.'' Dani giggled at his frown, held up her hands. "Teasing, just teasing. I have no basis for comparison. I haven't even been in your office. I don't get sick very often.''

No, she glowed like a beacon of good health, her youth and vitality making Luc feel far older than his thirty-three years.

"What about your brothers? Are they stubborn too?''

"Of course.'' He nodded. "But you can reason with them, if you can understand them.'' He caught her puzzled stare. "They speak an unknown language—at least to me. Computer mumbo jumbo. They're partners in a tech company in Arizona. I love them both, but a lot of the time I don't understand a thing they're saying. Mostly I just nod and slap them on the shoulder.'' He shrugged. "Works for me.''

She giggled at his silliness. "And your parents?''

He blinked up at her. "Hey, what is this? Twenty questions?''

"Just curious. But if you have something to hide, then—"

"I never said that." Luc knew perfectly well that one whisper of a secret in Blessing and he'd be under the microscope of every busybody in town. He resigned himself to explaining.

"It's just that I don't talk about my family much. My parents died when we were young. We lived with my grandparents." He decided that was enough information. "Okay, herein endeth the history lesson. Maybe we should get started memorizing those lines."

"If I'd known you were so eager, I would have suggested that ten minutes ago." Dani whipped out her copy of the play and grinned. "Where do you want to begin?"

"Truthfully? I don't *want* to begin at all. That's why I'm here. I was hoping you'd found someone else. You're sure there is no one?" His heart sank when she shook her head.

"I'm sure, Doc. There's no one else. It's up to you." Dani looked at him through her lashes. "The first line goes…"

He gave in then, reconciled himself to the torture of embarrassment that could not be avoided.

"Doc!" she squealed for the fifth time, ten minutes later. "Think about what you're saying. You can't 'pry the tattles.' It's 'try the paddles.' Say it again."

Luc tried, he truly did. But as time went on, and he thought more and more about standing in front of a bunch of people he knew mostly from their presence in his very private examining room, he simply got worse. His tongue twisted into knots that not even Dani's soft coaching could undo.

"Face it, I'm lousy at this. You have to find someone else." He lurched up from his chair and paced across the faded boards. "I'm simply no good when it comes to public speaking."

"Anyone can be good at it. You just need the right method." She tapped one finger against her bottom lip. "How about singing your lines."

He groaned. How much could one man take? "I don't think singing is going to help," he mumbled.

"It might help you loosen up if you focus on something else. Try this." She repeated the first of his lines in a catchy little melody.

Luc repeated the notes and words as best he could.

"Again."

She repeated that word nine times, but by the time he made it that far, she had both ears covered and was curled up in a tight little ball.

"Stop, Doc. Please, have pity on me and stop."

He stopped, immediately forgetting what he was supposed to say next.

Dani unwound herself, pulled her fingers from her ears and stood. Her eyes were huge.

"Look, Doc, no offense, but I think the singing is out. You are tone deaf." She blinked at him. "Come on, I'm hungry. Maybe eating will help."

She didn't sound hopeful. Luc didn't feel hopeful. He felt defeated and at the end of his rope as he followed her into the house.

"Why don't you just let Big Ed do it?" he mumbled, watching her bend over to peer into the fridge. The jeans she wore had a jagged tear just above her knee. All her clothes seemed to be in tatters. He wondered why.

She twisted to glare at him. "We can't have a cowboy English detective. It won't work." The fridge door slammed closed. Now she stood on tiptoe, stabbed one finger at something in the freezer. "Are you hungry?"

He shrugged, then nodded. Breakfast seemed a distant memory. Lunch—had he eaten lunch?

"What if we put some steaks on to grill while we try to think of another method. I studied acting in college. One course, anyway. I should be able to come up with something." She didn't wait for his agreement, but thrust a package into the microwave and set the timer. "Can you make a salad, Doc?"

"Are you kidding? I'm a genius at salad making. Piece of cake."

He accepted the ingredients she handed him and set to work slicing and dicing, hesitating only when he remembered the comment about her cooking. Just how bad was she? Surely no one could mess up steaks....

"I'll get some potatoes." Dani was gone for three minutes and returned with two fat potatoes. She lifted the meat out of the microwave, put the potatoes in, then glanced at him. "What if we recorded the words on a tape and you listened to them while you were sleeping at night?"

Luc shook his head, turned back to his work.

"It's a nice thought, Dani, but I'd be hesitant about wearing a headset at night. I'm usually on call. Besides, I freeze up in front of groups. The sooner you accept that, the sooner you can find someone else." He spread tomatoes over the salad.

She butted his arm, forcing him to face her.

"If you think your sister is stubborn, Doc, you're in for a surprise. I do not give up. Not ever. Not with this ranch, and not on that play. There is a way around everything. We just have to find it." She nudged a piece of tomato to the edge of the bowl with one fingertip. "Tomatoes on the side, not in, please," she ordered.

"I like them in." He pushed the tomato back. "And since I'm the salad maker, I get to say."

"Do not."

"Do so."

She smacked her hands on her hips. "For a doctor, you are very immature," she informed him, her green eyes dancing with fun. Then she snatched the steaks from the counter and stalked outside.

"Am not," he called after her, then grinned at his foolishness. Being with Dani DeWitt made him feel young, expectant, as if life might just have a surprise or two left to show him.

Which was crazy. Dani was a kid, barely out of college. He'd buried his grandparents, pushed his siblings through school, put his own life on hold until theirs were settled, and then finished his own training. In terms of life experience, he was Methuselah and Dani DeWitt was in kindergarten.

But knowing that didn't stop him from glancing over one shoulder before he picked up a wedge of tomato and, with a little snicker of delight, buried it under half a dozen lettuce leaves.

It had been a long time since he'd relaxed long enough to tease and joke. Maybe Dani was young, but she was also fun—and she was grilling the juiciest steaks he'd ever seen.

Luc could use a friend like Dani.

Chapter Three

"Lucas, my boy. What brings you into my bakery again today?" Miss Winifred peered at him over the rim of her bifocals.

She hated those glasses, he remembered. Complained that they made her nose stuffy. Luc wondered if she remembered she was still wearing them.

"I, uh, well...I need some help," he muttered, feeling his cheeks burn with embarrassment.

"Help? With what?" She deftly rearranged the doughnuts into a more attractive display, her fingers nimbly moving from there to the next tray in the glass case. "Well?" She stopped what she was doing to glare at him.

"Is something wrong, Miss Winifred? You look frazzled." It was true. It was also shocking. During the months he'd been in Blessing, Luc had never seen Winifred look anything less than calm and competent.

"If you're trying to flatter her, it isn't working." Dani DeWitt stood behind him in the doorway. "Most women don't like to be told they look frazzled, Doc."

She took a second look at the little baker. "Though I have to admit, it is true. Hey, Miss Win. What's up?"

To Luc's utter dismay, Winifred Blessing burst into tears. He hated tears. He scanned the room hopefully. Shucks. Dani was blocking the doorway. He was stuck here.

"If you must know, Furly and I had an argument."

He opened his mouth to ask a question, but Dani nudged him with her elbow, shook her head, her green-gold eyes flashing a warning.

"I'm so sorry. Here, why don't you come and sit down for a minute on one of these dainty little chairs. You need a break."

"What I need is to apologize." Miss Blessing allowed herself to be shepherded to one of the four café tables she'd installed last year. She sat down, dabbing at her eyes. "Furly Bowes and I have run this place together for thirty years. We've never argued even once, not until today. I yelled at her. She quit." She burst into a paroxysm of new tears.

Luc stared over her head at Dani, hoping he'd find some answers there. She shrugged her slim shoulders, pushed one fat black curl behind her ear and gnawed on her bottom lip, thinking. He hoped she would come up with something soon. Those sobs were getting to him.

"Miss Winifred, Furly loves you and she knows you love her. I'm sure she's hurting as badly as you are. Why don't you run over to her house and make up. Doc and I will watch things here for you."

He opened his mouth to protest, but Dani's black-fringed eyes flashed a warning he couldn't misinterpret: Be quiet!

"Would you?" Miss Winifred smiled. "Oh, you are

such dears. Yes, that's exactly what I will do. Poor Furly. It wasn't her fault at all. It's just that dratted oven. I should have replaced it years ago, but I thought I'd be retired by now, you see.''

"You can't retire. Blessing needs you too much.'' Dani frowned as Miss Winifred burst into new tears. ''There's something else wrong, isn't there.''

The gray head bobbed once, twice. "I didn't want to admit it, Dani, but this dinner theater thing has me tied in knots.''

Now this he could empathize with. Luc knew how she felt.

"What, exactly, is the problem?'' Dani sat down beside her and waited.

"Well, you see, to seat that many people is a strain on our church fellowship hall. Getting waiters to and from the tables will be almost impossible in the short time between acts, and the limited space only makes it worse.'' She sniffed pathetically.

"So we'll find a new hall,'' Dani said. "No big deal.''

"But the seniors' hall won't be ready in time. That fire was bad.''

"Miss Win, you've been worrying about this too much. Doc and I will check into things, see if we can come up with an alternative. But you are not to worry about it.''

Luc sat up straight. How had he gotten roped into this?

Dani wrapped an arm around the slumped shoulders and hugged. He couldn't help noticing how frayed her cuff was, or that she'd been less than successful at repairing a tear on the arm.

"Promise me there will be no more of this, Miss Win.

You tell me what you need and I'll see to it. I don't want you taking on the cares and woes of that project. You do enough.''

"Well, thank you, dear. That's very kind of you to say." Winifred stood, removed her spotted white apron and patted her hair. "Now I must go see Furly. I'm ashamed of myself." She bustled out the door without a backward look, her steps firm and determined.

"Looks like it's just you and me, Doc." Dani grinned. "Ever worked in a bakery before?"

"No. And I can't now. I've got to visit a patient."

"Really? Who is it?" She blinked at his frown, her clear skin glowing with some inner translucence. "Maybe I can help."

"It would be wrong for me to reveal a professional confidence," he muttered, wishing he'd stayed in his office instead of racing over to get Miss Blessing's help. If everyone in town did that, it was no wonder she was frazzled.

"So don't reveal any confidences, Doc. Just tell me what you need." She walked over to a coffeepot sitting in the corner, poured two cups and carried them back to the table. "Go ahead."

"There's a man," he began, trying to remember not to give too many details. "He's elderly and he lives alone. I'm concerned that he isn't eating properly and I was going to ask Miss Blessing to help me find a way to get him a healthy meal—at least once a day."

"I see." She chewed her bottom lip, eyes thoughtful as she swung one slim leg back and forth.

Luc forced his attention back to the subject at hand. Dani DeWitt distracted him too easily.

"He's proud, you see. It would hurt him to think I'd gone behind his back to ask for help."

"I get your drift, Doc." She grinned at him. "Obviously today is not a good day to ask Miss Winifred to work on this. She's a little stirred up, and in my opinion she needs a break from thinking about meals."

"What do you suggest?" He waited, knowing she'd come up with something. That was one thing he was learning about Dani—she always had an idea.

"I have a hunch we're talking about old Mr. Potter, aren't we."

"I never—"

"No, you didn't. And that's to your credit. But I've lived around here almost all my life, Doc. Nothing stays a secret in Blessing. Let me think for a minute."

She tapped one blunt fingernail against the table, obviously tossing around the possibilities. Her worn leather boots tap-danced their own rhythm against the ceramic tiles.

He frowned. This was taking way too long. He'd been so careful. Wouldn't the gossips just love seeing the two of them huddled together at Blessing Bakery?

"I've got to get out there. I promised to drop off his medication before lunch."

"Hang on a sec, Doc. I'm thinking as fast as I can."

Luc watched her glance around the bakery, saw the way her eyes lit when they rested on the individual meat pies chilling in the cooler.

"You've thought of something. What is it?"

"I don't have a long-term solution, yet. But for today, why not take him a couple of those potpies and one of those little salads from the grocery? You could pick up an apple or something for dessert, and maybe a quart of milk."

"I guess." It wasn't exactly the solution he'd hoped for.

"If you took three, you could eat lunch with him." She studied his face. "What's wrong with that?"

Luc tried to hide his reaction. "I—uh, that is, I don't know that I'll have time to wait while they heat up. I've got a clinic this afternoon."

Dani glanced at the clock.

"Miss Winifred's oven is empty by now. Let's pop three of them in and let them heat while we wait for her. Then there won't be any delay." She snatched three of the pies off the shelf and scurried into the back, returning with empty hands a few moments later. "Won't take long in that monster."

"I can't wait here, Dani. I've got work to do." Which wasn't exactly true. His last two patients had canceled this morning, which was why he'd agreed to take Mr. Potter's tablets out to him.

"Is there something you don't like about Blessing, Doc?"

Luc's head jerked back as he stared at her, only now realizing how tiny she was. Somehow Dani seemed like one of those people who were larger than life. She inspired thoughts of grandeur. Which was about as fanciful as a guy could get.

"Why would you say that?" he demanded. "I certainly never gave—"

"No, no." Dani brushed away his objections. "You never said a word. It's more the way you act. Take the church groups, for instance. I heard that you don't join in, haven't signed up to be on any committees, except for the dinner theater. Why, you even missed the pie social last week, and nobody in their right mind misses that!"

"I didn't realize it was imperative I be there. I'll be

sure to attend the next one.'' He couldn't disguise his sour tone.

"Keep that attitude and no one will give you even a sliver.'' She frowned and cupped her palm around her chin, elbow perched on the table. "What's with you, Doc? Why are you so afraid to get involved with us?''

"I'm not afraid. Not at all.'' Luc searched desperately for another subject, but nothing came to mind.

"Sure you are. In the social department, you act like a big chicken. Why is that? Have you got some secret you don't want us to know about?''

She was like a dog with a bone, relentless.

"I don't have any secrets,'' he insisted, wishing he'd never walked through the bakery door. "I just enjoy my privacy.''

"Uh-huh.'' Dani rose, dealt with a customer, then plopped back down beside him. "You've been in town long enough that you should be getting tired of your own company.''

He smirked. "What can I say? I'm an interesting person.''

"Uh-uh. Not buying that, Doc.'' She pursed her lips, narrowed her cat eyes and frowned. "How old are you?''

"What?'' He couldn't believe she'd asked that, today of all days.

"Your age, Doc. Forty?''

"Hardly!'' He was furious until he noticed the tic of laughter at the corner of her full lips, begging to be released. "Thirty—uh—thirty-four,'' he admitted.

"When's your birthday?''

Oh boy. "Why?''

She shook her black head, the curls dancing around

her cheeks as she tut-tutted at his prevarication. "When?"

When he didn't answer, Dani got up, walked to the phone and dialed. "Hi, Nicole. This is Dani DeWitt. Do you know when Doc—Luc's—birthday is? Sure, I'll wait." She twisted to face him, her eyebrows rising as she listened. "I see. Well, thanks so much. Very interesting. Yes, indeed. I will let you know. Bye."

"Dani, I—"

She waggled a finger at him. "If I were you, I wouldn't say another word, Doc. Your secret is out. Thirty-four today."

He sighed. "Let it go, okay. I saw what the town did for Joshua's birthday. Believe me when I say I do not want crows all over my yard. Not in the least."

"So what were you going to do? Pick up a cake and celebrate at home alone tonight?" She clucked her tongue at his guilty look. "Birthdays are meant to be shared, don't you know that?"

"Well…"

"You have friends here, Luc. Blessing folks would love an opportunity to wish you happy birthday and share in your special day, especially after all you've done for them in that clinic."

"I guess I'm not really into sharing," he muttered, embarrassed by her soft remonstrance.

"I wonder why that is."

"Why what is, Dani?" Miss Winifred waltzed through the door, her face beaming. She glanced from Dani to Luc, then shrugged. "Thank you so much for minding the store, my dears. I've had a word with Furly and the rift is mended. I'll make a special note to watch my cantankerous tongue from now on, you can be sure."

Her curious stare moved from Luc to Dani, then back to Luc, her forehead pleated in a frown of contemplation.

"Have I missed something?"

Dani shot to her feet. "Not a thing, Miss Win. Luc's going out to a patient's house to drop off some medicine. I'm going to show him the way. I popped three meat pies in the oven to warm. Hope you don't mind?"

"Of course not. Are you headed out to Gordon Potter's?"

Luc stood, shook his head in disbelief. How did these women know this stuff?

"I'm hoping you are because I made a banana loaf for him today. I don't make them often, but yesterday Dr. Darling mentioned something to the druggist about a refill while I was in there. I meant to phone him."

"We'll take it." Dani prodded Luc with her elbow. "Won't we, Doc?"

"What? Sure." *We?* He'd intended to make a quick trip out, to drop off the pills and something to eat for the man who shared his birth date. He hadn't intended the whole town to get in on the act. "I'd also like you to box up that small chocolate cake. I'll take it along too."

"Is it Gordon's birthday?" Miss Winifred checked a large white calendar on her wall and nodded. "Yes, it is. I'd forgotten that. Thank you for thinking of it, Luc. Gordon loves chocolate. Just let me write on it, okay?" She picked up a tube of bright yellow icing and wrote across the cake. "There now."

"Hey, Doc, why don't you pick up that milk and those salads from the store and meet me back here? It will take a few minutes to wrap up those pies so they don't get cooled off on the way out."

"No, it won't. I have—"

Dani began coughing loudly so that the rest of Miss Winifred's words were drowned out. He didn't need his medical degree to know it was a fake cough.

"Go ahead, Doc," Dani said huskily, patting her chest. "I'll meet you back here. We'll take my truck. The road out there isn't great."

And what was new about that? Luc wondered. None of the side roads around Blessing were in great condition.

"Fine. It will only take me five minutes," he warned.

"That's great."

He glanced from Dani to Miss Winifred, trying to decipher the strange looks passing between the two. It was no use. He'd never been good at figuring out that unspoken stuff. He pulled open the door and stepped outside.

By the time he returned to the Blessing Bakery, considerably longer than five minutes had elapsed. It was as if everyone in the small grocery store had conspired to delay him by chatting about the most inconsequential things. Luc shoved open the door, and stopped short when Dani's head popped up and Miss Winifred stopped midsentence.

"Are you ready?" he asked when no one said anything.

"Ready?" Dani frowned.

"Of course she is, Lucas. We just got gabbing and lost sight of the time. I'll pack those pies into my new Styrofoam boxes and they'll stay warm as toast." Miss Winifred bustled away, humming a little tune as she worked in the back room.

Dani folded a piece of paper and tucked it into her pocket.

"What's that?" Luc asked, curious about the bright red flush on her cheeks.

"Oh, just some notes I made about the dinner theater. Miss Win had some suggestions. Think I'll phone about the Baptist church hall."

"There we are. All snug as a bug. Aren't these carryouts delightful?" Miss Winifred held out three white packages. Thin red script spilled across one corner, spelling out *Blessing Bakery, made with love.*

Cute, Luc thought. "Very nice," he said.

"I do like a good design. And red is such a lovely color for a bakery. Vibrant and fresh." She picked up a square white box with the same inscription, tied with thin red cord. "Here's the cake. I know Gordon will enjoy it. I put the banana loaf in beside it. I hope there's not too much for him. He eats like a sparrow."

"I'm sure he'll want to save the loaf for tomorrow, but we'll help him with the cake." Dani waved and yanked the door open, waiting while Luc paid for his order. She fluttered a hand. "Bye, Miss Win."

"Goodbye, dears. Have a blessing day."

Luc rolled his eyes. A *blessing* day? Rolling over corrugated back roads in Dani DeWitt's clunker? Oh, yeah, it would be a riot.

In fact, it was. Dani teased Mr. Potter and he teased her right back. He was delighted with their lunch and ate every bit of his pie, gushing compliments for Miss Winifred left and right.

"That woman is a treasure. Too bad she never married. Cooks like a dream, you know." Gordon licked his lips when Luc lifted out the cake. "Oh my. Chocolate."

"Happy Birthday, Gordon. And many more of them."

"Ah, laddie, 'tis a blessed thing ye've done here." Suddenly Gordon Potter's Scottish burr was as thick as molasses. "I've no had a cake for me birthin' day since Hettie passed on."

"Then, it's time you did," Dani decreed, brushing her lips against his whiskery cheek as she wrapped her arms around his neck in a hug. She burst out singing "Happy Birthday," nudging Luc rather hard with one toe of her pointed boot, until he finally joined in, though he was careful only to say the words.

"Thank ye, me wee chums." Gordon savored a mouthful of the chocolate confection, eyes closed.

"If you can remember the words to 'Happy Birthday,' you can say your lines at the dinner," Dani hissed to Luc. "What's one person more, or less in the group?" She held out a plate with a thin slice of cake on it.

Luc stared at the minuscule portion and frowned. "Is that all I get?"

"I don't want us to eat all his precious cake, Luc. You heard him. It's been years since he's even had a birthday cake." She plunked the saucer on his knee.

"Ach, surely a lad the size of yerself needs a wee bit more than that, boyo?" Gordon lifted the knife to cut another piece.

"No, Gordon. But thanks all the same. This is the perfect size. I had a snack this morning and it's not sitting too well." In truth, Luc had missed breakfast and was starving, but he'd gladly forgo the cake if it got Dani's warning glare off him.

Luc had barely scraped the last creamy smear of icing off his plate when the alarm on his watch beeped.

"Gordon, it's been great to visit with you. I wish you a very happy birthday. But I'm afraid I've got to head back to town. I've a patient scheduled in half an hour." And considering Dani's driving on the way out here, he was going to be late. Tortoises moved faster than her tired old truck. And they certainly had better upholstery.

"Yes, we've got to go. But will you come over to the Double D tonight, Gordon? Someone sent over a lemon pie this morning and I can't possibly manage it all myself."

Why didn't she ask *him* to share her lemon pie? Luc wondered. But Dani did not extend the invitation to him, though he hinted at it by telling them both how much he liked pie, especially lemon pie.

"It'd be an honor, Dani. Seven-thirty?"

"Perfect." She nodded, grinned, then turned on Luc. "Come on, Doc. You've goofed off most of the morning. Back to work for you." She scooped up their debris and dumped it into a garbage pail, closed the cake box, and set it and Gordon's prized banana loaf in the fridge.

Luc barely had time to shake the old man's hand and wish him happiness before Dani had him in her vehicle, speeding down the road. Gone was the tortoise of two hours ago. Now she sped over the road, twisting and turning the wheel like a professional race-car driver. As Luc's lower back teeth met his uppers for the hundredth time, he could only hang on and hope they made it back to Blessing in one piece.

She squealed to a stop in front of his office. "There you go, Doc. Right on time."

"Th-thank you," he managed to say, easing his aching bones out of the truck. Was he actually thanking her for that bone-crunching ride?

"Listen, Doc." She leaned across the seat, chewed

on one lip, then finally looked him in the eye. "If you really think you dare to eat at my house, you're welcome to show up any time after I finish chores. We could go over your lines again, I suppose."

"Ah—" He'd been all set to agree until she'd added that last part.

"Or we could just eat pie and celebrate your birthday." She chuckled at the relief he knew was telegraphed across his face.

"I could bring out a pizza for dinner," Luc murmured.

Her face blanked, then grew very pink. "Uh, no. That won't work. Sorry. Seven-thirty would be better, the same as I told Gordon. I eat early. It takes me a while after that to get the horses fed."

He nodded. "Oh. Okay. Thanks. I'll see you later."

"Sure." She pulled the door closed and revved the engine. "See you later, Doc."

Where she'd previously dawdled, Dani DeWitt now spun away as if chased by hounds. As he walked into his office, Luc wondered if he'd ever understand the way a woman's mind worked. No doubt his sister could answer that, not that he intended to ask her. Some things should be left for God to fathom.

Dani sat in the kitchen and waited, then flicked the porch light on when she heard the quiet purr of his car, anticipation sending the butterflies in her tummy into a peculiar version of *Swan Lake*. She hoped she hadn't made a mistake.

He stopped beside her truck, cut the engine, turned off the lights. She pushed open the door and stood on the porch, watching.

"Hey, Doc. You're a little late."

"I know. Sorry." He climbed out of his car and raked a tired hand through his hair. "A late patient."

"One good thing about lemon pie," she told him as he climbed the stairs, "it keeps."

"I guess. Gordon's not here yet, I see." He stopped, stared at her sprigged cotton sundress. "You look nice."

Dani laughed.

"For a girl who works in the barn so much, I clean up okay," she giggled, watching red flood his face. "Thought your birthday deserved better than my ripped-up jeans. I've seen your eyes glitter when you look at those tears," she teased. "I imagine you must be itching to stitch them up. Nicole offers every time I see her. Come on in." She held the door open, waited for him to walk inside.

He did, took a seat at the table.

"Uh, no, not here. I thought maybe we'd have coffee and pie in the den," she told him. "Just go through that door. I'll bring everything in."

"Can't I carry something?" He hesitated, one hand on the swinging door.

"No. You go ahead. I'll be there in a second."

"Okay." He pushed the door open, then froze as a bunch of voices began a rousing rendition of "Happy Birthday."

Dani grinned, enjoying his confusion.

"Happy birthday, Doc," she whispered, standing on her very tiptoes so she could reach his ear. "Some of your friends stopped by to share our pie. Hope you don't mind."

His eyes told her he knew exactly what she'd done. His fingertips were white against the door as he listened to them sing. Dani held her breath, hoping he wouldn't be angry.

"They just want to be friends," she whispered, pressing her hand against his arm. He stared at her for several moments before he finally nodded and released his death grip.

"It's very, er, kind of them."

"Come along, Lucas. Blow out these candles before this cake becomes a wax statue." Miss Winifred took over, ushering him into the room in front of a huge cake decorated with many, many candles.

"How many girlfriends has the lad got?" Gordon Potter cried out, thoroughly enjoying the ruse.

Dani watched Luc glance around the room and note the grinning faces that smiled back at him.

"Thank you all very much," he murmured. "I'm... shocked."

"We have that effect on people sometimes." Big Ed stepped forward. "Blessing folks get a little carried away." The room erupted in laughter.

"Blow, Luc. I want a piece of that cake," Joshua Darling called out.

Luc blew.

"Mercy, open those windows, Dani. It's like a pea-soup fog's descended on us with all that smoke." Miss Winifred handed Luc a knife. "You cut, I'll plate."

Dani began the coffee rounds, ensured the punch was ready and found chairs for two more latecomers. The sound of laughter rang through the old house, bringing it alive as it must have been long ago, when her mother lived. It was good to hear. The house had been empty too long.

She hovered in the background, watching as Luc moved from group to group, his sober smile relaxing a little more with each encounter. By the time he came to the end of the line and shook Gray McGonigle's hand, he looked almost completely at ease. That was a start.

Gray held up his hand for silence.

"Luc, we're mighty glad you're a part of our town and it's a real pleasure to share this day with you. We know we've kept you pretty busy over the past few months while Dr. Darling was laid up."

Muted laughter testified to his understatement.

"We brought a few things we figured might help you relax."

"There was no need—" Luc accepted a strangely wrapped package from Big Ed. "Oh. Thank you," he murmured, then tore away the paper to reveal a hammer.

"Man wants to build things, he needs tools." Big Ed grinned.

Everyone clapped.

"Marissa's and my gift will go with that." Gray handed him a flat, rectangular box. Inside were dozens of Band-Aids in assorted cartoon characters. "Have you ever seen him with a hammer?" he asked the rest of the room, tongue in cheek. "'Physician, heal thyself' seems appropriate advice."

Luc flushed at the good-natured gibing. "I just need practice," he mumbled.

"Uh-huh." Gray looked unconvinced.

"Now, this is something you can really use." Joshua and Nicole watched proudly as their daughters presented Luc with a brand-new fishing rod. "Just don't phone in sick when it's our day off."

"Deal." Luc brushed his fingers over the shiny green surface. "This is too kind of you," he said.

"Well, we ain't done, so don't start bawling just yet." Gordon Potter hooted with delight. His own countenance shone as he sat surrounded by gifts he'd been presented with before Luc arrived. "The best is yet to come. That's what I tell myself every year."

The members of the cast lugged a huge picnic basket to the front of the room.

"Frozen dinners," they told him. "You bake one whenever you're too tired to cook."

"Hmm, competition." Miss Winifred frowned, waggled her eyebrows at the group. "I don't think I like the way this party is heading."

"No competition, Miss Win." Dani stepped forward and hugged her. "You outdo all of us. Just look at this gorgeous cake."

"Well, I did have a little something else." Winifred lifted a huge pickle jar and set it in Luc's arms.

"Uh, thank you," he muttered, puzzled. One finger scratched through the paper she'd wrapped around the glass.

"They're buttons," she told him with a wink. "I've noticed several missing from the front of your shirts lately. These are replacements."

Dani held her breath as his face got very red. He kept his eyes on the jar for a long time. Finally he looked up, and his broad shoulders were shaking. She let her breath out. He wasn't angry, he was enjoying himself!

"It's the most unique gift I've ever received," he told the older woman, and hugged her.

"Thought ye might get some use out o' the likes o' this, laddie." Gordon held out a piece of newspaper.

Luc reached out and accepted the paper, his eyes on the old man's face.

"One of your own lures, isn't it?" he murmured as

one finger rippled over the feather attached to the hook. "I've heard about these from several expert fly fishermen. Thank you very much, Gordon." He patted the man's shoulder awkwardly.

Gordon reared back as if he'd been stung. "Dinna get sentimental wi' me, boyo. Not with these lassies watchin'."

More laughter.

Content to remain in the background, Dani handed out cake and refilled cups as one after another of her guests brought something they'd fashioned especially for the doctor. The laughter lasted well into the night. Then, one by one, the guests wished Luc well, thanked her for the party and headed for home.

Last to go, Miss Winifred insisted on tidying up before she left.

"It's not right to leave you with the mess, dear. Though I'm glad enough we chose paper dishes. No washing up." She tied the garbage bag closed with a flourish, hugged Luc, then snatched up her purse.

"You won't have much sleep tonight, Miss Winifred," Luc said. "Not with your early mornings. But I want to thank you again for the wonderful cake. I've never tasted better."

"You have plenty of leftovers. That should tide you over for desserts." Miss Winifred hurried out the door. A second later she poked her head back in. "And I'm to sleep in tomorrow morning. Furly's orders. She thinks I've become a little cranky." She wrinkled her nose, sniffed, then giggled like a young girl. "Bye, dears."

"Bye. And thank you." Dani closed the door behind her, smiled at Luc. "You're not mad at me?"

He frowned. "I should be."

"Oh." Dani winced.

"But how can you be mad at someone who's just hosted the entire town at your birthday party?" He grinned. "I guess I should be glad you didn't sprawl my age across the cake in black numbers."

"Yes, you should. I was sorely tempted." She fiddled with a few unused dishes, then met his stare. "They really just want to be your friends, Luc. They won't push or pry. Well, not much, anyway. But they're there if you need them."

"I'm beginning to realize that." He took the dishes from her, set them on the counter, then took her hands. "Thank you, Dani. It was very thoughtful of you to do all this."

"I enjoyed it." She smiled. "It's been a long time since this house was filled with happy people."

"I thought you said you weren't lonely, way out here."

"I'm not. I just enjoy having people here, laughing." She dragged her hands away from his, then lifted one hand to her lips. "Oh, I forgot!"

"We stuffed ourselves with cake, ice cream, punch and coffee. What could you possibly have forgotten?"

He was looking at her the same way her father sometimes had. As if she were young and foolish. Dani didn't like that look. Young and foolish women didn't have the responsibility of a ranch dumped on their shoulders. She preferred strong, independent, capable. She drew herself up to her full height—all five feet three inches of it.

"I just meant I forgot to give you your gift." She pushed through the door, searching for the small red package she'd spent ages hiding in just the right place so she could lay her hands on it easily. "Here it is." She gave it to him.

"You shouldn't have done this, Dani. The party was more than enough."

She smiled. "Open it."

He did, then quickly glanced up at her as his fingers trailed over the worn, red leather cover, traced the entwined embossed gold-colored letters.

"RLS. Robert Louis Stevenson's *Treasure Island*. Where did you find this? It's very old."

"I know. It was my father's, given to him by his grandfather who received it when he reached his twelfth birthday. Do you like it?"

"I love it. Old books and I have a special relationship." He blinked at her, eyes wide. "But I don't think you should give a family heirloom away."

She blushed in embarrassment. "Don't be silly. Who better to give a book to than someone who enjoys it? I hope you do."

"Dani, you've given me more than enough. I didn't need anything else." His dark eyes seemed to melt as he stared into hers.

"You mean the party?" She shook her head. "That was different."

"Different? How?" He sank down on the sofa, crossed one knee over the other and leaned back, his craggy face perplexed.

"I just wanted to show you that you're part of the community here. There's no need to keep to yourself or stay away from things. Folks in Blessing love adding another one to the group."

"It's very kind of them."

She caught the hesitancy in his voice. "But you don't

want to be included, is that it?'' Dani frowned. She peered down at him. ''Did I make a mistake tonight?''

''The party was a wonderful idea. And I appreciated it. Really.''

''But?'' What was wrong? There was something Luc wasn't saying, something that obviously bothered him about the situation.

''Dani, I don't know how long I'll be here.''

She frowned. ''But, when you didn't leave after Joshua came back to work, everyone thought that meant you were staying.''

''I might. He and Nicole have offered me a place in their partnership. I'm just not sure yet.''

Something in the way he said it finally twigged. Dani frowned as she put her thoughts into words.

''So until you have decided, you don't want to invest yourself in this community?''

''That's not exactly what I meant.''

''Close enough.'' It made her angry. What did he have to lose? No one was trying to hog-tie him into anything. Well, no one except her. She needed him in that play.

''Dani, I—''

''So that's what's behind all your excuses.'' Indignation vied with frustration. ''You think that you can come here, live among us for almost a year, and not become part of us? That you can just walk away if you decide Blessing isn't the place for you?'' She shook her head. ''How can you do that, Doc? How can you avoid commitment like that? Don't you want roots, to settle down among people you know and trust?''

''Yes! Of course I do. I'm just not sure this is the place for me to do that.'' He clamped his lips together as if he'd said more than he had intended.

As far as Dani was concerned, it was more than enough.

"So what are we—on trial?" She snorted her disgust. "You'll take whatever we offer, but if we get too close, if someone asks more of you than you want to give, you'll brush us off and leave?" She smacked her hand against a cushion, fluffing it harder than necessary. "I was right. You are a chicken."

"You don't understand," he muttered, leaning forward, one hand fiddling with the hem of his pants leg.

"Then, explain it to me, Doc. Make me understand why you'd run away from the friendship and hospitality of the kind of people who came here tonight." She faced him head-on, dared him to tell the truth.

"I don't know if I want the responsibility being part of this town entails," he blurted out in frustration.

"What? That doesn't make any sense. Why?" Dani refused to back down. "Tell me why."

He glared at her but she ignored the anger. Something was behind this, and for some reason she had to know what caused his reticence.

"You want the truth?"

She nodded.

"Fine. I spent my childhood being responsible, Dani. Because my parents weren't. I spent another five years being responsible after my grandparents died. I'm responsible for my patients, for paying astronomical medical school bills, for every piece of advice I give. I don't want any more commitments."

Dani stared at him, the silence of the room no longer friendly but oppressive. She shook her head.

"No one's asking you to commit anything, Doc. They just want to be your friends. Do you even know what that means?"

"It means they'll expect me to be there if they need me. I can do that, in a medical context. I just don't know if I want to do more than that."

She sighed, sat down on the sofa, and stared at her feet and the toenails she'd painted with such high hope for this evening. So much for glamour. "Maybe you need to think about why you came to Blessing in the first place," she suggested, confused by his words. He was perfect for their town, he fit in. Why couldn't he see that?

"I just came to help out."

"That's a commitment, Doc," she whispered. "One of the biggest you'll ever make."

"You don't understand."

"Sure I do." She stood, smiling at his startled look, then walked toward the door. "Here's your cake. You'd better take it with you. It's late. I've got an early morning coming. I took the liberty of carrying your gifts out to your car earlier. Good night, Doc. Happy birthday."

"Yeah, I need to get going. Good night." He walked to the door, pushed it open, then turned back. "It was a great party," he said.

"Which you didn't want." She closed her eyes and leaned her head back against the wall. "I'll try not to interfere in your life again, Doc."

"Dani, I—"

She didn't want to hear it. She'd messed up. Again. When would she learn? "Good night."

Silence. Then a faint *swish* that told her he'd left. The screen door to the kitchen banged shut as if to reaffirm that.

Dani stayed where she was and looked at the balloons and streamers she'd hung so happily just a few hours earlier.

"I was just trying to be a friend, Lord. Just a friend."

But Luc wasn't looking for friends. He didn't want to get involved. Which made all her efforts tonight look pretty foolish. Once again she'd trusted her heart's first inclination and misread everything.

Dani curled up on the sofa, hugged her knees and let the tears fall. Suddenly being alone seemed just too much to bear.

Chapter Four

"As a rehearsal hall, the church is fine. But we've got to find somewhere suitable to stage the play, and we've got to do it soon. It's important that the actors be able to gauge how loudly they need to speak. If we change the venue later on, I'm concerned that there won't be enough time to adjust words and movement. It has to look natural."

Luc froze, his hand raised to knock on the pastor's half-open door. Everyone, including him, knew he was the least natural actor up there. Was Dani worried about his performance? Worried enough to find someone else?

"I know I threw a lot at you when I asked you to handle this, Dani. But the truth is, you're good at it and you bring out the best in people. Your group *wants* to make this a success for those kids in that orphanage. We'll just have to pray harder that somebody cancels their reservation. The Baptist hall would have been perfect."

"I know it." She sounded defeated. "I have been

praying, Pastor, probably more lately than I have in my entire life. But the answers aren't coming.''

''The ranch situation is pretty bad?''

''Worse than I ever imagined.''

The minister's softly voiced question and Dani's sad response floated to Luc in the hallway. He turned to leave. It wasn't right to stand here and eavesdrop, even if he already knew Dani DeWitt was up to her eyeballs in debt. That was her private business.

He wandered back out to the sanctuary, flopped onto a pew and studied the huge tapestry hanging above the pulpit. The work was unusually vivid, the depiction of Christ on the mountain, speaking to the five thousand, visually compelling. He knew it was titled simply *The Teacher,* and that someone in Blessing had created, then donated it. The ''who'' was a mystery the entire town shared.

Too bad God didn't give me the gift of public speaking. Maybe then I'd be able to meet her expectations.

Luc rubbed the back of his neck, trying to ease the tension that tightened across his shoulders every time the subject of the dinner theater came up. Why was it so hard to say those lines? What made him stutter and stammer over a few easy-to-pronounce syllables? He knew them by heart, could see them engraved behind his eyelids if he closed his eyes. So why couldn't he say them?

''You don't want to invest yourself in this community.''

The memory of Dani's words stung. He'd avoided her for the past two weeks, except for practice. If she'd asked, he'd have pleaded busyness. It wasn't a lie. He was always busy. But Dani hadn't asked. Neither had she laughed and chatted with him as she had with the others. She was outwardly friendly, but focused and businesslike, her attention centered on the play.

And he hated it.

Luc was surprised by his intense reaction.

He'd enjoyed the flash of interest in her eyes when her attention got snagged on something and she burst out laughing. He'd liked the way she was open and genuine with him. But lately she'd hardly laughed at all, let alone shared anything.

Was it because he'd rejected her friendship, or did it have more to do with the ranch and the problems she'd inherited? Would she cut him more slack if he really dug into the part of inspector?

A hand on his shoulder jerked him from his introspection. Dani stood beside him frowning.

"Are you all right, Doc?"

"Of course. Why wouldn't I be?" He told himself to control the belligerence. Dani wasn't the problem. He was.

"I dunno. You've been staring at that hanging for ages." She tilted her head back, checking to see if he'd found some flaw. "Hadn't you noticed it before?"

"Yes, I noticed—" He cut himself off, swallowed and regrouped. "I guess I got lost in my thoughts."

She nodded, sank down beside him.

"I can understand that. This is a good place to think."

She was nervous, fidgety, her feet scuffing over the floor. Luc felt a little tense himself, on edge. Shouldn't he, as a doctor, know how to ease her worries?

That was ridiculous. He barely knew Dani DeWitt.

"Have you got a lot to think about, Dani?" he asked softly.

Her head jerked so she could stare full into his face. After several moments, she nodded.

"We've got to find a location for the dinner theater."

"I know. But it's not just that, is it." He hoped she'd open up to him, if only to ease the burden he sensed she found too heavy. He was good at listening. He'd sat through Millicent Maple's babbling stories for entire evenings. In fact, most of the elderly in Blessing seemed to home in on him for a chat.

"What else is bugging you?"

She smiled at his choice of words, her hand automatically shoving a mass of curls behind her ear. Her eyes glowed with that mysterious light that came from inside—from her heart.

"*Bugging* me, Doc? Is that your medical term for a specific ailment of the mind?"

"Of course." He grinned right back, his heart picking up speed. This was the Dani he preferred, the one who wasn't afraid to reach out and grab onto life. The one who made him feel considerably younger than his thirty-four years. "What's up?"

She laughed. "That should be my line, Doc." Then the smile melted away and her face lost its glow. "The ranch. What else? I seem to spend every waking hour putting out fires."

"Something's burning?"

She laughed, shook her head and rose. "No. Just another way of saying that I'm barely handling the crises. Anyway, I don't want to unload on you. Do you have time for a coffee? I have to wait another half hour for some welding to be finished."

"As long as the coffee comes with one of Miss Winifred's doughnuts. I'm a sucker for her bakery." He followed her down the aisle and out the door. "Since your truck's being worked on and I didn't bring my car, I guess we walk.''

"Do you good. Sitting in that stuffy office all day can't be healthy…for an old guy like you." She ignored his raised eyebrows, held out one brown arm so her skin lay next to his. "Look how pale you are. A little fresh air, some hard work, and we'll make a man out of you yet, Doc." Her eyes dared him to take up her challenge.

Luc stared at her, then made up his mind.

"I'll race you to the bakery." He didn't wait for an answer, but took off running as fast as he could. Several seconds passed before he heard the clatter of her sandals on the sidewalk behind him. Luc didn't look back and he didn't slow down, in spite of the strange looks he got from the citizens of Blessing who graciously stepped aside to allow him to pass.

Thankfully, the bakery was empty. He managed to drag himself to one of the small chairs and flop into it, chest burning, breathing ragged and uneven.

"Lucas? What on earth—?" Miss Winifred scurried out from behind the counter, her blue eyes wide. "Is something wrong?"

"Water," he gasped. "And coffee and a doughnut. Please." It was all he could manage. He concentrated on filling his starved lungs.

"Well, of course, but—"

The door jerked open and Dani rushed inside, her face bright red, her tousled curls bouncing with every step she took. She looked like a cheerleader in her cut-off shorts, long, tanned legs strong and shapely. Her white T-shirt was streaked with dust where she'd wiped her forehead on the hem. Her chest rose and fell rapidly as she advanced on him.

"That…wasn't…fair," she panted. "Head start."

She dropped into the chair opposite him. "Can't run in sandals." She grabbed the glass of water Miss Winifred carried and took a long drink.

"I'll get another glass for you, Luc. And two coffees, was it?" Winifred looked from one to the other, noted their breathless state and shook her head. "Like two young kids," she mumbled. "Furly, have you ever seen such a thing?"

Furly emerged from the back room, took one look at the pair of them and burst out laughing. She was still chortling as she hurried back to her beloved baking.

By the time Miss Blessing returned with their coffee and Luc's glass of water, Luc was almost certain he could manage a whole sentence without puffing. Not bad for an *old man* like him, was it? Just to be sure, he took a sip of the water, then inclined his head at Dani.

"Who were you calling old?" he asked, one eyebrow lifted in what he hoped was haughty disdain.

"You." Dani lifted the glass from his hand and drained it. "You run like a girl," she muttered, mopping her face with a napkin. "May I have a jelly-filled doughnut, Miss Win?"

"Yes, of course." It was clear that Miss Blessing had more to add on the subject, but something prevented her.

Luc watched her faded blue eyes regain their sparkle and knew something was going on in that wily brain. His warning radar clicked on, but he wasn't exactly certain what it was telling him, so he kept his eyes on the older woman.

"I'll go you one better," she murmured. "I've just finished a fresh batch of my love cookies. I'll give you each one of those."

"Thanks." Dani grinned. "We need sustenance after

our race. Luc won, but he cheated. Still, he is a lot older. I suppose it's only natural that he'd need an advantage. And my sandals aren't really made for running.''

For once Miss Blessing's mobile face did not communicate her thoughts. She glanced from one to the other, nodded, then bustled away, mumbling something about perfection under her breath.

''She's awfully quiet.'' Luc didn't think that was a good sign when it came to the baker.

''Tired, I expect. She and Furly have been working on a rather large wedding cake. That would wear me out. Just the thought of piping all those little rosettes and I'm a nervous wreck.'' She shuddered. ''Give me the ranch any day.''

Miss Blessing returned with two plates. On each one a large, lightly browned heart rested. Vibrant red-icing letters adorned the top of each.

''They look lovely, Miss Win.'' Dani broke off the bottom point of the heart and slipped it between her lips. ''Melt in your mouth.''

''Thank you, dear. I do hope the words are of some value. I don't know exactly why, but they came to me just a few minutes ago.'' Miss Winifred smiled archly, then brushed her hands over her pristine white apron. ''Please excuse me now. I have to finish that cake. Why a wedding cake must include a waterfall is anyone's guess.''

She called to Furly, muttering something about over-indulgence. After rather obvious glances over their shoulders, the two disappeared a moment later.

''They're up to something.'' Luc knew he was stating the obvious, but he had to make Dani aware that their baker was contemplating more than a wedding cake. He knew that look, had met up with it before, in other towns where he'd filled in. Every town had a least one matchmaker, and he was pretty sure Miss Winifred was Blessing's.

His gaze fell to the cookie. His eyes widened.

The 1st gift is life. Love is 2nd, understanding 3rd.

"I'm not sure I understand exactly what this means," Luc murmured, checking over one shoulder to be sure Miss Winifred wasn't listening. He'd expected some mildly romantic phrase. But this was…well, different. Maybe he'd misread the woman?

"She likes to make them cryptic sometimes, to make you think. Look at mine. *Live by what you trust, not by what you fear.*"

"I can understand yours," he told her, then caught the skeptical glance she directed his way. "Well, sort of. It's an encouragement. You trust God, you live by faith. I think she's talking about your troubles on the ranch." Luc studied the hearts, then nodded. "Yours is easy. But what does mine mean?"

Dani nibbled on the unwritten edges of her cookie, her eyes on his.

"Understanding will come later?" she guessed, a grin sliding from her mobile mouth to her gorgeous eyes. She shrugged, studied him. "You think?"

"Maybe," he muttered doubtfully. "It's a bit like figuring out those fortune cookies we get with Chinese food, isn't it."

"Don't let Miss Winifred hear you say that!" She checked to be sure the wily baker hadn't yet returned. "She says she is inspired by God. And after seeing how on-target she usually is with her advice, I can't dispute it."

"You're right, of course." Luc shrugged. "Maybe we'd better ask for the translation, then." It took about two seconds to rethink that. "On the other hand, I believe I'll mull on this for a while." He glanced up, decided to take the risk. "Her advice to you is exactly what you need."

"Really?" Ice frosted around the edges of her formerly friendly tone. The sparkle drained from her eyes until they seemed shuttered and sad.

"I don't know exactly what your situation is with the ranch, Dani. I'm sure I wouldn't understand even if you told me. But I do think there must be a purpose in your trials. If you can hang on long enough, God will make the path clear."

She bit her lip, her eyes turbulent. Luc held up a hand.

"I know I should mind my own business, that I'm sticking my nose where it doesn't belong. But I have to say this anyway—don't let it get you down, Dani. Hang on and keep trusting. Something good has to come out of it. Remember, 'all things work together for good.' It just takes a while, that's all." He hoped that sounded encouraging. She'd given him so much, he just wanted to give back a bit of hope.

She said nothing out loud, but her eyes told him a lot. Dani DeWitt took her job seriously. Right now, he was pretty sure she was in over her head, but even if she told him what was the matter, Luc knew he wouldn't be much help. He was a city kid, born and raised. Horses and ranches were way out of his league.

"I'd better go," he mumbled, glancing at his watch. "I told Joshua I'd take hospital rounds tonight since I've had a couple of hours off this afternoon." He swallowed the last of the cookie and washed it down with his cooled coffee. "If you want someone to talk to or a shoulder to lean on, I'm around."

He wasn't sure about that last part, especially since he had no intention of getting involved.

Dani gave a quirky grin. "Why, Doc! Are you offering to be my friend? You who wanted to stand back and test the waters in Blessing?" She raised one eyebrow, waiting for his answer.

He deserved the question. He had been standoffish, even though Dani had nothing to do with his reservations about getting involved. Even if he did end up leaving the little town, he'd leave behind a friend he could remember happily. Wasn't that worth a little effort on his part?

"Yes, I guess I am," he told her sincerely. He thrust out a hand. "I'd be honored to have you as a friend, Dani." As her fingers curled around his, Luc caught a glimpse of Winifred reflected in the glass. She was smiling.

"It's always good to make a friend," he said loudly, knowing full well that Miss Winifred would see the word in an entirely different light.

Dani frowned, nodded, then pulled her hand away.

"Yes, it is," she replied, just as loudly. She studied him for a moment, shrugged, then moved to the door. "I've got to get going. It gets dark early these days."

"Does it?" He peered out the window. "I thought the days were getting longer."

"They are." She giggled. "I meant it gets dark before I can get all the work done. C'mon. I'll walk with you."

He waited until they were outside on the sidewalk, alone. Then he reached for her elbow. "Uh, Dani?"

"Yes?" She stopped, frowned. "Okay, what's wrong now?"

"Nothing's exactly wrong. Back there—" He jerked

his head toward the bakery. "I really did mean I'd like to be your friend."

"Yes, I understood that. Thank you." She was distracted, waving at a passerby who had called her name. She twisted around to look at him. "Was that everything?"

"You don't understand." He waited until he had her full attention. "Friendship is all I'm offering. I don't want anything more."

She didn't look away then. In fact, her entire attention was on him, and it made him shift uncomfortably. When she finally spoke, her words were quiet but full of meaning.

"You really are a chicken, aren't you, Doc. You extend one hand to me, and use the other to push me away." She shook her head. "I don't pretend to understand what's just happened in the peculiar workings of your mind, but I promise you, I'm not looking to you as a way out of my troubles—or for anything else, for that matter. I've learned to depend on myself. I'll manage just fine on my own. I always have." She walked a few steps away from him, then turned. Her cheeks glowed bright in her anger. "I think I've figured out the last part of Miss Winifred's love cookie."

"Really?" He watched the fire burn in her eyes and knew, with a pang of regret, that he'd hurt her feelings. "Why don't you tell me?"

"You make a lot of assumptions about what people want from you, Doc. Understanding seems to come last. Too bad. I bet you miss out on a lot by being so prickly."

Then she turned and walked away, her sandals slapping against the pavement in a tattoo of condemnation.

When she'd disappeared from sight, Luc sighed, shook his head, and headed for his car.

Now he'd done it. And by the looks of Dani's ram-rod-straight back, it wouldn't be easy to wiggle his way back into her good graces. He needed a plan.

As he drove back from the hospital later that evening, Luc cast a glance at the bakery, considered, then tossed the idea out. No, apologizing to Dani had to be done on his own, without coaching from anyone. Besides, Miss Winifred was bound to get the wrong idea about his concern for Dani's tender feelings. Miss Win wouldn't understand that he'd seen something in Dani's eyes that told him she needed a friend, someone she could trust. She certainly wouldn't understand that he'd botched his offer of friendship by putting conditions on it, conditions that Dani in her self-imposed exile didn't need.

He wasn't sure why all of it mattered so much; he only knew that it was important Dani knew he liked being with her, that he truly wanted to help.

"Why me?" he groaned, turning up the drive to the little house that was, for now, home. "Why am I such a flop when it comes to relationships?"

It wasn't so much that the answer eluded him. It was more that he didn't want to think about it.

That evening Dani slogged her way through her usual Friday-night stack of chores, trying with little success to keep her mind off Lucas Lawrence. As if to frustrate her, his car appeared in her front yard just as she left the barn.

"Hi," he said, his eyes wide as he assessed her dirty appearance. "Is this a bad time?"

"Depends." She wasn't going to get slapped down again. Dani stood and waited for an explanation.

"A bad time to visit, I meant. I was hoping you could spare me an hour or so to go over these lines. With the first full practice tomorrow, I don't want to embarrass myself any more than necessary."

He looked so downcast at the prospect that Dani had to chuckle. "Is it really so bad?"

"Yes." He followed her across the yard. "Put yourself in my shoes. I think I'm moderately intelligent. I managed to get through medical school okay. I can treat almost any case I get in Blessing, or find someone who can, but I can't master these lines in public. It's—"

"Humbling?" she murmured, glancing up.

"At the very least." He saw her smile and shook his head. "It's not nice to laugh at me," he told her, his voice prim and proper.

"I know. But it's so much fun. And out here on the ranch, we take any kind of entertainment we can get."

She led him inside, then excused herself while she went to clean up. By the time she returned, Luc was flipping through an old volume she'd unearthed from her father's room last night.

"Do you have any idea what this is?" he demanded, his eyes glossy with excitement.

She nodded. "Henry Van dyke."

"Yes, but it's a first edition!" His hand caressed the worn and tattered cover. He opened the book tenderly. "Listen to this. 'Who seeks for heaven alone to save his soul may keep the path, but will not reach the goal; while he who walks in love may wander far, yet God will bring him where the blessed are.'"

"It's beautiful, isn't it?" Dani smiled. "I found that tucked in the pocket of the big chair. Dad must have been reading it before he...died." She turned toward the refrigerator, made a production of searching its contents.

"I've never seen this title before. Is it any good?" He turned the book over, as if the answer lay on the back cover.

"It's interesting. It's the story of the other wise man." When she received no response, Dani turned to find his attention centered solely on the book. She grinned and went on with her supper preparations, adding another egg and a little extra ham and cheese to her omelette, just in case he wanted to share.

She arranged two plates with tomato slices, toast and half of the omelette, then set them on the table. "Wake up, Doc. It's supper time."

"Dani, I didn't come for supper." He set the book on a side table, out of harm's way.

"I know." She nodded. "But I thought you might want to share mine. Besides, I hate eating alone." It was true, but she could see he didn't believe her.

"Thank you."

"You're welcome." She said grace, then poured them each a cup of tea. "It's an omelette," she told him, irritated by the way he poked his fork into her creation.

"Ah. Isn't an omelette supposed to stay in one piece?" he asked, cutting through it with his fork. "It looks like scrambled eggs and vegetables."

"Then, that's what we'll call it." She lifted a forkful of the food to her lips and ate it, trying not to grimace as the charred bits of egg stuck to the roof of her mouth. "More toast?" she offered.

"No, thanks," he muttered, easing his plate away. "I, er, had supper before I came out. Hospital food."

He blinked, then rushed to cover his gaffe. "Nothing near as good as this," he told her. "Leftover stew and some rice pudding."

Dani sighed. "You don't have to pretend. I know I'm not much of a cook. But I get hungry and eggs are healthy, though I don't usually burn them."

"The tea is very good."

She gathered the dishes, scraped what was left into the garbage. After rummaging through the cupboard, she found a container and offered him some cookies. "Don't worry. I didn't bake them. Miss Winifred left them after the party."

He took three. So much for not being hungry.

"Do you want to start on your lines now?"

"No."

She glared at him.

"Well, it's the truth. I don't even want to think about those lines. But I suppose I'll have to do it anyway. I promised Miss Winifred I wouldn't wimp out. Everyone else is putting their whole heart into this play. I don't want to let them down." He dunked the cookie into the tea and rushed it to his mouth before it crumbled. "I love doing that. My grandmother would slap my fingers if she saw me."

"Was she very strict?" Suddenly Dani couldn't stem her curiosity about his childhood.

"A tyrant." He grinned, remembering. "But she was also very caring. We always knew she loved us. Gramps, too. They kept all of us on after my parents died. Never seemed to have a qualm about raising three kids."

"Kept you on?"

"It started out as a temporary situation. Mom and Dad were tour leaders and they began to realize that it was easier to make a living with the overseas tours. We stayed with Gran and Gramps while they were gone.'' He must have seen her curiosity, because he offered the answer before she could ask. ''They died in a plane crash.''

''I'm sorry.''

''Thanks.'' He shrugged. ''I probably felt their absence more than the others. They were younger and had spent most of their time at Gran's.''

''What did your grandfather do?''

''He was a doctor. I was going to take over from him as soon as I finished my residency.''

''A family practice.'' She smiled. ''Continuing the dynasty. I like that.'' But Luc hadn't done that. Instead he'd come to Blessing to fill in. ''What happened?''

''When I was in medical school, my grandparents were in a car accident. My grandfather was bringing my grandmother back from a chemo treatment.'' His voice was quiet. ''They were both killed on impact, which was a mercy. My grandparents thought the sun and moon rested on each other. They hated being separated. I couldn't imagine either one of them without the other, and I certainly didn't want Gran to suffer.''

He was making their deaths sound so...acceptable. What wasn't he saying?

''You said you were the eldest? The others must still have been in school.'' She looked for the emotion on his face and found none.

He nodded. ''Yes, they were.''

''Well? What did you do?'' She grew impatient with him. She was fascinated by his story and wanted to know more, but it was like pulling hen's teeth to get him to talk.

"I left school and took over as the parent," he told her. "Is there any more tea?"

She poured the amber liquid into his upraised cup, her brow pleated in a frown. "But you were in school. Don't doctors in training work all kinds of crazy hours?"

He nodded, sighed at her glowering look. "You want the whole story?"

She nodded.

"I left school. My parents weren't wealthy, though they had some life insurance. My grandparents had a few dollars tucked away, but not enough to pay for college for all of us. I closed up Gramps's practice. We sold the house, packed up and moved to Texas. I went to work in the oil fields."

A deepening surge of affection clenched her heart as she realized that he'd given up his own dream to get his siblings through school.

"But you're a doctor now. You must have gone back to school."

He nodded. "It took a while, but I did finish."

"And since?"

"I've filled in for other doctors who needed a break, worked the emergency room for a couple of years. Then I came here."

Dani understood what he wasn't saying. He hadn't decided to settle in Blessing, he was just passing through. But she didn't understand why.

"Do you like it here? Is Blessing Township the kind of place you could set up a practice like your grandfather had?" It was probing and she knew it, but she wanted to hear him admit that he was afraid to settle down.

"I like it very much." At best, the answer was non-committal.

"But?"

He laughed. "I think that's enough about me. Why don't we turn the tables, Dani. What about you? How come there's no one hanging around, waiting to help you out with this ranch?"

"Like a man, you mean?" She scrambled for a way to avoid answering. "I don't think I'm the type men hang around."

"What does that mean? What's wrong with your type? You're very pretty, you're smart and you're ambitious. What more could a guy want?"

"You tell me."

She hated him probing into her past like this, hated the way he reminded her of just how inadequate she was. Most of all, she hated the compliments. Did he mean them, or was it just offered as a sop? When had she become so poor at reading people?

"Come on, spill it."

Dani closed her eyes, sighed. She'd stuck her nose into his business. Turnabout was fair play.

"There was a man, once. In fact, I was engaged," she muttered. "It didn't work out."

"You were engaged?" The doctor frowned, obviously trying to recall. "Funny, Dermot didn't mention it. Before Christmas I saw him almost every day. I'm sure he never said a word about you getting married, though he talked about you a lot."

"Dad didn't know. I broke it off before Christmas."

"Ah." He nodded, understanding rippling through his dark eyes. "And you wanted to get away during the holiday and nurse your wounds. That's why we couldn't reach you. You were hiding."

Dani chewed her bottom lip in frustration.

"I wasn't hiding—not a broken heart, anyway." It still stung that she'd been so betrayed. How was it possible to know someone so well, and yet not know them at all? But then, even her own father had fooled her into believing all was well. Evidently she was lousy at gaining the trust of people she cared about.

"You were hiding from him, is that it?" He considered it, then nodded, answering his own question. "Your pride was injured by this guy and you needed some time to get it together. I see."

"No, you don't see at all," she burst out, the anguish still eating at her soul. "He stole my creation, *my* work. And he passed it off as his own. He lied and cheated and pretended to care about me, just so he could steal from me. I trusted him, thought he actually loved me for myself. What a joke! The only thing he loved about me was my work."

"What did he take?" Luc asked, his brows drawn together. "Did you report it to the police?"

"No. I confronted him, thinking he'd have enough decency to admit he'd done it." Anger burned as she remembered that awful day. "Brad denied that he'd stolen anything. He said we'd simply happened upon the same idea and he'd developed it better than I had. He claimed I was jealous of his superior talent."

"But surely you had the work to show you'd written it?"

"He'd copied everything, put his name on it. I had no way of proving anything. I'd planned to enter that project in a scholarship program that would have paid for my graduate work. My professor was going to look it over during the Christmas break and give me his critique. Before I even comprehended how far his deceit had gone, Brad had already entered my pl—work, under his own name.''

''I'm sorry.'' His quiet offering went a long way to soothing her angry spirit.

But he couldn't understand how much that play had meant to her. How could anyone appreciate the hope she'd invested in it? For two years she'd secretly written and rewritten the words, honing each line to knife-edged perfection. It would be her ticket onto Broadway. Every spare moment out of class had been spent investing her energy in a dream that Brad had shattered irrevocably.

She had trusted him so blindly, she hadn't seen it coming.

''It doesn't matter now,'' she told Luc, rousing herself from the past. ''I'm not going back. There won't be any graduate work. I belong on the Double D. I never should have left.'' She let her gaze slip over the familiar items in the kitchen.

There was the maple work center where, at fourteen, she'd tried to make her father a cherry pie. It had been terrible, hard as leather, but he'd eaten it without hesitation and told her it was delicious. And there, at the end of the counter by the stove, the burn mark where she'd once placed an overheated pot and nearly set the cabinets on fire. The linoleum floor was scuffed and marked beyond recognition, but she always pretended that with enough scrubbing, she could restore the glossy sheen—make it look like those magazine pictures.

What was one play compared to all these memories?

''He'll get his, Dani. What you dish out always comes back to haunt you later in life. Don't let it get you down.''

''I'm not,'' she assured him, lying through her teeth. Her biggest regret loomed large. ''Still, I wish I'd told

Dad where to reach me during the holidays. I wanted to come home, but I knew he'd figure something was wrong and that he'd want to help. He couldn't have done anything, of course, but that would have made him feel worse. I was so staggered by Brad's betrayal that I wouldn't have been able to hide my feelings, and that would have upset Daddy. Still, if I'd come back, maybe then…''

She let the words die away. She had accepted that she couldn't go back, couldn't rewrite the past, no matter how much she wanted to. But the hurt remained.

''The thing is, Dani, God had a plan too. In His divine scheme, it was time for Dermot to go home. Your being here wouldn't have changed God's timing.''

''You're right, of course.'' She surged to her feet, grabbed her copy of the play from the phone stand and flipped to the first page. ''Let's get to the play, shall we?''

He gave her a searching look. Dani met it, tried to look unconcerned. Why had she blabbed all that? He didn't need to know the story of her life. It only made her vulnerable, and she hated feeling like that. Vulnerable people got taken advantage of.

She held herself still, pretended she was fine. After a moment, Luc shrugged, retrieved his copy and began scanning it. But mere moments later, he slapped it down on the table.

''Dani, I have to tell you something. I lied. I didn't really come out here to practice lines with you.''

''You lied?'' She stared at him, unwilling to believe it. But the truth was there on his face.

He nodded, his eyes brooding and dark. ''I actually came out here for another reason entirely. It has to do with the ranch.''

"The ranch." She didn't get it. Why lie about that? Why lie at all?

"I know I should have told you straight out, but I thought you wouldn't listen. I thought you'd toss me out on my ear for interfering."

"Interfering in what?" She wished she could think up an excuse that would get her out of here, give her a minute to consider what he was saying, to organize her thoughts. But Luc was right here and he wasn't waiting for her to offer more of an opening than she already had. "What do you mean?"

"Interfering in the ranch." He held up one hand when she opened her mouth to speak. "I know it's none of my business. But you're working so hard, and from what I've heard, there's not a lot you can do to save the place."

"Is that right? No doubt you've discussed this with those who would know." She made herself say the cutting words, forced herself to pretend she wasn't mortified to her boots. "Why don't we just stop dancing around the truth. Why are you here, Doc? Really."

"Gray McGonigle's brother is back and Gray is going nuts trying to keep him busy so he won't go running off again. He's kind of a hard case."

She nodded. "I know all about Adam's gambling. What's it got to do with me?"

"If you could come to some arrangement with Gray, maybe Adam could run the Double D. Rent it, or something."

Embarrassment and indignation rose inside at the thought of discussions on coffee row she could only guess at, but Dani forced her voice to remain steady.

"I can't just hand it over. There are a lot of debts. I want to see them paid off. It's what my father would have wanted.'' She decided to stop the verbal fencing. ''I know what everyone thinks. I know what they're saying. They think this is too much for me. They think I should declare bankruptcy and walk away, let the bank sell everything.''

''I'm not sure—''

''I am. That's what all this concern is about, isn't it? The rest of the county would pick up my father's stock and land for peanuts and I'd walk away with nothing.'' She pinned him with her eyes. ''That is what you're suggesting, isn't it?''

''Well, something like that, I guess. Though I don't imagine your friends and neighbors would ever relish knowing you were in trouble. I wouldn't like to see you go, either.'' He had the grace to blush with embarrassment. ''I just thought—maybe it would make things easier for you.''

''Easier? To abandon my home?'' She stood, moved toward the door in a pointed gesture that should have told Dr. Luc Lawrence that she wanted him out. ''Uh-uh. Sorry to disappoint you, Doc, but that isn't going to happen.''

He rose too.

''I didn't mean to offend you, Dani. I just thought—''

''You thought what? That I'm the kind of person who runs away from her problems? That at the first sign of hardship I'd give up? You thought wrong, Dr. Lawrence.'' She opened the door and hung onto the handle, quelling her anger and frustration. ''I'm not about to walk out on the one thing my father left me. I know it won't be easy, I know I'll have to scrape long and hard to get this place out of the red, but that's exactly what I'm going to do.''

The indignation she felt could be contained no longer.

She glared at him. On second thought, before he left, she was going to have her say. Maybe he'd pass it on, and the rest of the town would stop gossiping about her private business.

"I don't appreciate this at all. Anything I told you was in confidence, not meant to be shared with all the busybodies on coffee row. The last thing I want is for every nosy Parker in Blessing to discuss my business. I would have thought that, as a doctor, you could respect that."

"I didn't talk to anyone about it," he insisted. "Not to anyone. It was just something I heard, and that triggered some thoughts—"

"I can guess what you thought, what the whole town thinks. It's not very pleasant to be the local charity case, you know. It's embarrassing and demeaning, and I would prefer it if you would find some other topic of conversation with your friends." She shoved her toe against the screen door so that it opened a few inches, then slapped back against the frame, waiting for him to leave.

Luc didn't move.

"I'd like you to go, please. I have things to do. I'm sure someone as educated as you can learn a few lines without my help."

His mobile face couldn't hide his thoughts. He was mad, frustrated and a little bit ashamed. But she wouldn't let herself feel sorry for him. He had deserved every word she'd said.

Luc wasted two minutes glaring at her, then stalked across the kitchen and shoved the screen door open. He stepped outside and let it slam shut behind him, but before Dani could close the inside door, he was back, his face two inches from hers.

"There's a certain double standard operating here, isn't there, Dani? It's okay for you to tell me to get involved with the kind and generous people in this community, to not be so irritated when everyone pokes their noses into my business. You insist people in Blessing just want to be my friends." He laughed harshly. "Well, guess what? The same thing is true for you. You're trying to shut yourself away here, hide out while you lick your wounds, pretend everything is exactly as it was. You're afraid to let anyone see the truth, but all your friends want to do is help."

"I am not hiding." The very idea made her seethe. "I'm trying to juggle a lot of things at one time. I'm busy. And this is my personal concern. I am not some community project charity case."

"Is that how you think of the others, when they need a helping hand? Is any needy soul just a charity case to you? It's okay for them to need help, but not you?" He shook his head. "Nobody's glorying in your misfortune, Dani. In fact, they're worried about you. They'd like to help, but you push everybody away."

"This is something I have to do on my own," she muttered between gritted teeth.

"Says who? You won't let them share your troubles, just like you wouldn't let your dad comfort you when it would have given him the greatest pleasure to do just that. You cheated Dermot of that, Dani. Just like you're cheating your friends of any blessing they might get out of being there for you. Is your pride really worth so much that you'll cut yourself off from everyone who tries to help?"

She could say nothing, could do nothing. How could he understand?

Luc stared at her for a long minute, then sighed,

turned and walked to his car. He paused a moment, waited, as if he hoped she'd say something, but when she didn't, Luc nodded.

"I wasn't pretending to be your friend, Dani. I meant it. But friendship takes two. The next move is up to you." Then he climbed into his vehicle and drove away into the night.

Dani stood watching him, her heart in her throat, as she called herself a fool for allowing herself to trust her feelings.

"How many times will it take before I learn to stop trusting?" she hissed into the night.

Dark storm clouds thundered in the distance. She sniffed the air, caught the scent of rain and sighed. Mending fences was never fun in the rain, and she had miles of rails to repair tomorrow.

"The next move is up to you."

She had told him things she'd never told anyone. She'd trusted him to understand how much she needed to prove herself, and he'd told her to dump it all, to walk away.

Dani frowned. Wasn't Gray a good friend of Luc's? Was that why he'd come running out here with his idea, to help Gray? Was it okay to kill her dreams if it helped his friend?

Bitterness welled up. *Pull back, Dani. Don't lead with your emotions. Think things through.*

As she sat in the kitchen, ordering her brain to function, Dani couldn't help wondering, how much trusting the wrong person would cost her this time.

Chapter Five

"Hello, Dani."

Luc acted as if that scene last night at the ranch had never happened. Fine, she would too.

"Hi." She pretended to organize her notes.

"Have you told her yet?" Miss Winifred bustled up, her arms filled with clothes.

Dani stared at the garments, then remembered the rummage sale to be held on Monday afternoon.

"Not yet." Luc lifted the bundle from the older woman's arms and set it on a chair. "I thought you might like to be the bearer of good news."

"Me? But it's your idea." Miss Winifred frowned at him, then shrugged. "Well, I can't wait any longer. Dani, we've got our dinner theater location. If you agree."

"Really?" Dani stared at her. It was about time something went right. "Where?"

"At the park. Luc was telling Albert Pert about our little problem and Albert suggested the forestry department's camp presentation building. Their naturalists do many presentations during the summer, of course, so the building is well used. But if we want to be part of their schedule for the summer, we can. Here are the dates he suggested.'' She held out a calendar with a red circle around the last three days of July.

"But that's too soon. Since we weren't having much luck in finding a hall, I assumed we'd hold off, present it in the fall.''

"There are some advantages to the summer date.'' Luc's quiet voice drew her attention. "Not that I want any more audience, you understand. I'm nervous enough. But maybe performing in front of strangers would be easier. And the park is bound to be full of potential customers.''

"All we have to do is tell Albert whether or not we want the place and pay the damage deposit.'' Winifred clasped her hands together, her voice rising with excitement. "Best of all, they'll include our production with the newsletter they send out in a month. Anyone who is planning to come to the park will be able to buy their tickets ahead of time. We'll know well ahead whether we can meet our goals.'' Her blue eyes shone with anticipation.

"It does sound good,'' Dani admitted, privately wondering how in the world they could possibly stage this production in such a short time.

"Those windows have the most spectacular views. We can string little lights outside to add a mysterious effect. What do you think?''

"I think it's a wonderful setting. But I don't remember a kitchen.'' Dani refused to look at Luc. Had he seen through the bravado in her voice? "Can you manage without a kitchen on site, Miss Win?''

"I keep forgetting you've been away. Last year they

added a kitchen. The camp received a grant and some forward-thinking board member convinced the group that they could host a Christmas celebration out there as a fund-raiser for their programs. It's absolutely perfect for us."

"Okay." There was no way Dani could fit in a trip to check out the facilities for several days. She decided to trust Miss Winifred. Surely she wouldn't let her down.

"If you're satisfied, then let's go with it. There's certainly plenty of room in that hall."

"Yes, there is." Winifred turned to Luc. "Did you ask her yet?"

He shuffled, avoided Dani's glance. "I don't think Dani wants—"

"Why don't you let me decide what I want," she told him pointedly, then turned to Winifred. "What's the problem?"

"Albert invited Luc to go out with him on the trails, but Luc can't ride. I thought you might teach him."

"Me?" She did look at him then. "Why not Gray? You and he are friends."

"Gray is, um—he's got his own problems right now."

Dani blinked. "I thought his spread was doing fairly well. Does he have trouble? Maybe I can do something to help."

Luc's eyes lost their sleepy look. They honed in on her, glittering black ice chips.

"Do you think he'd want charity?" he murmured, his tone brimming with meaning.

Miss Winifred glanced from one to the other, picked up her bundle of clothes, then excused herself.

Dani watched her scurry away, then glanced back at Luc.

"It's not the same," she told him quietly.

"Isn't it?" He raised one eyebrow. "I'm afraid I can't see any difference."

"I didn't deliberately go out of my way to poke my nose in Gray's business." *Like you did,* she wanted to add.

"I didn't do that, Dani. I was only trying to help." His lips thinned, communicating his frustration. "Besides, though you've tried to hide your problems, no one in this town is blind. Everyone's seen trucks leaving the Double D with your father's stock. They're not stupid. They can guess what's happening." His features hardened until she could read no emotions on his face.

"Yes, I suppose they can." She'd admitted that to herself last night, along with a few other things. Admitting that her pride had been hurt had been hardest of all. "Why do you care?" she demanded, glaring at him. "Not one week ago you were prepared to sit on the sidelines of our town. Now all of a sudden you're acting just like one of the busybodies."

"I wasn't sitting on the sidelines. I care, okay? Maybe it's just that I don't like to see you hurting," he said, fiddling with the costumes someone had left behind. "Maybe I wanted to help."

"That's getting involved," she told him.

His gaze held hers; he nodded once, face solemn. "I know," he murmured. "You said I wasn't committed to anything. Well, I'm committed to making this play a success. I don't know why you want me involved, but I'll do the best I can."

So what did that mean? That he also wanted to get involved in Blessing? That he intended to stay?

Or was it just her he was interested in?

Her heart picked up a beat and she immediately told it to be still. Why would he be interested in her? Besides, Lucas Lawrence wasn't someone she could allow herself to care about. Not if he was going to walk out of town when the next good offer came along.

Suddenly aware of the others milling around them, Dani straightened, reined in the questions she wanted to ask.

"Maybe we'd better talk about this another time," she told him. "The others are here for practice."

"Sure." But he didn't look away.

There was a flicker in his eyes, a glint of black determination that told her he wouldn't be put off as easily as before.

"Fine," she said.

"How about lunch after church tomorrow?"

Dani frowned at him. "Lunch? Why?"

"To build on the friendship we started. I meant what I said, Dani. I do want to be your friend. I guess we need to work out what the conditions of that friendship will be."

The sincerity in his voice touched her deeply, until she remembered he'd insisted he wanted nothing more than friendship. So there, she told herself. There was nothing to get excited about after all. Anyway, she didn't have time or the inclination for more than that. Trust took time to build, and she didn't believe Luc would be around long enough to make her forget the past.

Neither would she, unless she got the Double D out of hock, and soon.

"Well?" He stood waiting, one foot tapping impatiently.

"Fine. Lunch after church. On one condition."

"Which is?" His eyes sparkled with fun. "Marvin joins us?" he guessed.

"No. It's much simpler than that."

He waited, one eyebrow arched.

"That I don't have to cook. You bring lunch with you out to the ranch. After that, we'll get started on your riding lesson." She answered his grin with one of her own, then told herself to stop acting like a silly teenager.

Luc was years older than her and miles beyond in experience. All he wanted was a few lessons to help him stay upright on a horse.

Fine. She could do that, and she'd keep it strictly business.

"Okay, people." She clapped her hands to get their attention. "Everybody on stage. We're going to run through this thing from beginning to end if it kills us."

"And it just might." Luc sighed heavily.

Dani handed him the notebook she'd brought. "Pretend you're studying your notes," she whispered. "Your lines are here. Don't lose your place. A smart man like you can handle that, right?"

"Ha!"

She'd hoped to goad him into forgetting the audience. And for the first act it worked. He was the consummate bumbling inspector she'd visualized when she wrote the play. The second and third acts weren't nearly as well done, but Dani still felt a tingle as she drove home later that night.

Hope. That's what it was. She felt hope. It had been a long time coming.

"Horses don't like me," Luc told her as the old nag she'd told him to climb onto thumped over the green-tinged hill, jiggling him around in a manner nothing like the smooth fluid movements he'd seen other riders exhibit. "At least, this horse doesn't like me."

"Don't be ridiculous. Flower likes everyone. But you keep pulling on the bit and it hurts her mouth. She definitely does not like that. You have to relax and let your body move with the animal."

"I *am* moving with the animal." He winced as a specific portion of his body made contact with the saddle, then glared at her. Flower—what a dumb name for this ugly horse.

"No, you're not, Luc. You're trying to brace yourself for what you think is coming. Flower's done this before, she knows what to do next and she won't throw you. Stop expecting the worst."

It struck him that those were words he needed to remember. How had he come by the habit of always expecting God to dump on him? Was that how he actually saw God the Father—as a malicious ogre just waiting to crash his world?

"Come on, I want to show you something."

Dani made a strange noise with her teeth and her horse took off galloping. Flower had obviously followed Duke more than once, and on this occasion apparently refused to be left behind. She ran, if you could call this odd-gaited rhythm running, jogging Luc in the saddle as if he were no more than a sack of oats. Which is exactly how he was beginning to feel.

"Uh, Dani—" he called as his body shifted to one side and he began a sliding descent toward the ground. "Help!"

She was beside him in an instant, her strong brown arms hauling him upright.

"What happened?"

What *had* happened? One minute he was sitting there, the next the world had shifted. He felt the metallic taste of dread in his mouth and refused to give in to it. She would not see it. He'd already humiliated himself in front of her with the play. There was no need to repeat the experience.

"Luc?"

"I'm fine." He dragged his aching body back onto the horse.

After giving him a clinical glance, Dani vaulted onto Duke with an ease he envied. She looked like every man's dream, perched on the big powerful stallion, her Stetson tilted back on her head, black curls framing her beautiful face.

"Okay. If you're sure?"

"I'm fine," he muttered as he tried to find some comfortable spot on the worn saddle. Wasn't leather supposed to be supple? "She just seemed to shift suddenly and I guess I lost my balance."

Dani surveyed his posture and shook her head. She clicked her teeth, and when Duke moved to stand next to Flower, she reached out to uncurl Luc's fingers from the horse's mane.

"You dropped the reins," she told him, a smile kicking up the corners of her lips. "That probably spooked her a little. And Flower doesn't like anyone to grab her neck. She's a little sensitive, so she wheels her head around. That's probably what did it." She handed him the leather reins. "Are you sure you want to do this?"

"Yes."

Dani shrugged. "Okay, well, we can take a break soon. This is my favorite spot. Right over there." She pointed, then moved Duke where she wanted, five-hundred feet away. With grace and elegance, she dismounted, then hurried over to help him.

Luc would have liked to climb off himself, but recalling Flower's dancing hooves from earlier, he waited until Dani was crooning in the horse's ear.

"Thanks," he muttered, when both feet were safely on the ground. Almost everything he owned protested—and he'd only been riding for twenty minutes.

"You have to see this, Doc." She dropped Flower's reins and hurried up the green swell of the closest hill.

"Won't they run away?" He followed her, twisting to check that his ride home was still around.

"Duke will come when I call. Flower doesn't like to be left alone, so she'll trail along behind. Just look at this." She spread her arms wide as if to embrace the vista before them. "Isn't this worth a little discomfort?"

He climbed the slight hill to stand beside her and stared at the panorama beyond.

"I hadn't realized we'd increased our elevation so much," he said. He glanced behind and saw that the farmhouse lay on lower ground behind them. But the spectacular view in front of him would not be denied. He took a deep breath to absorb the beauty of hills newly furred with green grass that sloped down below them to a meadow of delicate purple-blue flowers. A stream trickled through the center vee of the hills. "It's gorgeous."

"Yes, it is."

The quiet pride in her voice told him how much she loved this land. No wonder she wasn't prepared to part with it without a fight. He shifted slightly so he could watch the expressions flit across her face without staring.

"Sometimes I can hardly believe I've been away, that

Dad won't come racing into the house and yell at me to help with a foal.'' She dashed the tears away. ''I miss him a lot.''

''I know.'' There was nothing to do but listen. Maybe that was all she needed from him.

''This is my secret place,'' she told him softly, folding herself down on the ground, legs crossed in front of her. She patted the grass beside her, waited until he sat down, then continued speaking.

''I used to come here a lot whenever I was upset or angry or just needed time to think. I'd ride out here, lay on my back and stare into the sky. Somehow it seemed like God waited here, all ready to listen to me.'' She looked to see if he understood.

Luc nodded. Though he'd never experienced exactly that, he could imagine the solace she found out here.

''It was like we had a special place where we met, which no one else knew about,'' Dani went on, face tipped into the wind. ''Whenever I come here, I always feel reverent, sort of like I'm walking into a corner of the world where nobody else matters. It's not just that I could say anything here, pour out my heart and soul and not be ashamed. It was more that after I'd finished, I could hear better, I could understand what He wanted to tell me, feel the encouragement and love bathe over me. I called that feeling heaven's kiss.''

He let her speak, content to listen to her memories. Gone were the bland, meaningless words she usually employed to hide her feelings. Now she spoke glowingly of her childhood on the ranch, of the things she'd learned, of the father she adored.

''That was one thing I never found at college—my own secret hideaway, though I sorely needed it.'' She closed her eyes, savored the smells, sounds.

Luc watched her, content to let the silence stretch between them.

A few minutes later her big green eyes met his.

"I'm sorry, I must be boring you." Her cheeks pinked. "I didn't mean to go on and on."

"I wasn't bored." He wondered if Dani realized how much she changed when she let go of her inhibitions. Her eyes sparkled with life, her skin glowed with a translucence that came from more than mere good health. Her whole body moved and shifted as if she could barely contain a boundless energy.

"You're just being nice." Dani sprang to her feet, strode to the precipice and stared down.

Luc's heart lodged itself in his mouth until he saw how nimbly she chose her steps, testing each section of ground before she put her weight on it. She conducted her life like that, too, he realized. But today she'd forgotten the caution she usually employed with him. She'd seldom voiced her inner thoughts, seemed to keep them bundled away inside where no one could question—what? Her weaknesses?

Suddenly Luc realized that what he'd categorized as her fear of getting too personal had its roots in a lonely childhood. Living way out here with only animals and a crusty old man had made her self-reliant. She'd at least had her father to run to then, but she had no one now. At least, no one who could understand what drove her to hang onto this place in the face of what he'd heard were staggering debts.

Perhaps he'd just been given a glimpse of what made Dani DeWitt tick.

Luc moved to stand beside her.

"Dani?"

"Yes?"

"Are you okay? I mean really okay?" He deliberately stayed near enough to grab her should she stumble.

"I'm fine."

She turned her head to smile at him, and his heart began to race. Her Stetson hung by its laces against her back so that the wind twisted and pulled her mop of curls into a dance of joy. She looked young and carefree, as if the future lay before her waiting to unfold its bounty, just as the valley below exposed its own. For this moment at least, Danielle DeWitt had no problems. She reveled in her life. And he wondered, what it would be like to share her future?

Then she giggled. The sound brought him back to reality with a sting. She was young, he felt so old. And when she had settled her affairs, she'd go on, build a new life. Their futures did not lie together.

"What is it, Luc?" Her eyes darkening with questions, one hand reached out as if to stir him. "You have the strangest look on your face."

Saved the indignity of whatever muddled speech might have escaped, Luc felt a ridiculous gratitude for the crack of lightning that streaked across the canyon just then. There was little time between it and a loud clap of thunder. He turned, caught sight of the black thunderhead darkening the sky behind him and automatically scanned the area for the horses.

Duke stood nearby, pawing the ground to express his disquiet, his head lifted into the wind. Flower pressed against his flanks, her own nostrils quivering as she snorted her nervousness.

"Come on, Doc! By the looks of that sky and the speed it's moving in, we'll have to make a run for it."

He followed, racing across the grass as the ominous sounds of a storm crackled all around them.

"We're not going to make it back in time," he yelled, grabbing Flower's reins as she vaulted onto Duke.

Her grin of pure mischief dazzled him.

"Where's your faith, Doc?" She crouched over the stallion, ready to take flight. "Ready?"

He nodded once, and she took off. Luc wasn't at all certain of Flower's ability to keep up to the other animal, but the mare surprised him by galloping behind Duke with more speed than he'd imagined her capable of. He could do little more than hang on and pray Flower knew what to do.

The ride was exhilarating. They flew across the land, up and down hillocks, with the wind tearing at their clothes. The storm increased its warning menace as it chased them home. The rain began when they were still three miles from the big farmhouse, mere spatters of moisture at first, cool, refreshing. Then it came down in blue-gray sheets, drenching the countryside. By the time they arrived at the barn, Luc was soaked.

"Are you okay?" Dani asked as she slipped off Duke. "That lightning was getting pretty close and I didn't like to stop and ask."

"I'm fine. Just surprised I didn't fall off. I take back everything I said about you, Flower. You run like lightning." He patted the horse's neck, then followed Dani's lead, completing the tasks step by step as she explained each one. He removed all the riding gear, dried off the horse, then accepted the brush she handed him. He watched her, then implemented the same long strokes she used to curry the glossy coat. Safe now, Flower stood contentedly, offering only the tiniest whinny to tell him when he was too harsh.

Luc glanced around the stable, saw the empty stalls.

"What about the other horses? Don't we have to get them?"

She shook her head. "There are only five left and they know enough to stay someplace warm and dry, probably an old cave we used to call McArthur's Hideout. Horses are very smart." She took the curry comb from his hand, set it on a shelf. "That's enough. We'll give them some oats, then we'd better get ourselves inside and dried off. I can't afford to get sick, and summer storms are notorious for causing colds."

She clucked at Duke, brushed a kiss against his velvet nose, offered each horse a carrot, then turned to Luc. "Come on inside. I'm sure there is something of Dad's you can wear until your own stuff dries."

Luc followed her to the house, trying to dodge the worst of the growing mud puddles as he stifled his laughter. Dermot DeWitt had stood over six foot six and weighed well above two-fifty. Luc figured he'd have to roll up the pants four or five times, cinch in the waist about a foot. It wouldn't be pretty, but right about now, warm sounded awfully good.

She was right about courting illness. Sitting around in these wet clothes wouldn't be terribly bright.

"Come on in. I'll see what I can dig up."

Inside, she hung her coat on the peg by the door, stepped out of her muddy boots, then scooted out of the room as if she remembered the last time he'd been here.

Luc remembered it, also. Too well. This time he wouldn't make the same mistake. He'd mind his own business and preserve their tenuous friendship as best he could. Besides, how she ran her life wasn't his business. Strictly friendship, wasn't that what he'd told her?

"Here you go. Try these." She glanced at him critically, then pointed toward the bathroom. "You'll probably have to use your belt to hold them up. Go on and shower. After you've changed, I'll put your stuff in the dryer."

He nodded, realizing how chilled he'd become. Fortunately the shower was deliciously hot. When he was finally warm, Luc pulled on her father's clothes, adjusted them as best he could, then grimaced at his reflection. He took his wallet and keys out of the pockets of his pants, rolled everything in a ball and tossed it inside the dryer as he walked past on his way to the kitchen.

To his surprise, Dani wasn't there. But the delicious smell of a pizza baking drew a growl of anticipation from his empty stomach. He peeked into the oven. Ah, store bought. She couldn't do much to that, could she? A little extra cheese, maybe, but that was it.

"Luc? I'm in here."

He closed the door guiltily, glancing over his shoulder. She couldn't possibly have seen him snooping.

"Come on in whenever you're ready. I've got a fire going."

A fire sounded great. He walked through to the next room, then realized she was in the study beyond. One glance through the big picture window told him the storm hadn't abated. Wind snapped the branches against windowpanes now drenched by rain. It wasn't the first time he'd been surprised by a Colorado storm. He remembered Miss Winifred's words: *"If you don't like the weather in Blessing, wait five minutes. It will change."*

It didn't look like this storm was ready to end its fury just yet.

"I'm here."

She sat cross-legged on the floor in front of the fire, her wet hair curling around her head like a halo. The room was obviously her father's office. There were shelves all around. But oddly, many books sat on the floor. It was as if someone had been rummaging through them, searching for something.

"What happened here?"

"Don't mind the mess." She patted the carpet beside her. "I've been sorting through some of Dad's stuff. He had a number of old books and I thought I'd take some to an auction. A bookseller in Denver said he knew a man who was looking for some first editions." She waved a hand. "Feel free to browse."

First editions? Luc whistled silently as he walked over to a pile of darkened, discolored leather bindings that bore marks of much use. He squatted, trailed his forefinger over their spines, relishing the feel.

"You have a whole library of old books, and you didn't think to tell me before this?" He brushed his fingers over tattered red calfskin with reverence. "I love old books." He scanned the titles, assessed the gilt on the pages and chose what he thought was the oldest, then checked inside for the date. "Ah, 1826," he whispered.

"That's my pile of the oldest ones I've found…so far." Dani waved a hand at the bookshelves that surrounded the fireplace. "Of course, I haven't had time to get to those yet."

"But where did he get them all?" There were bookcases on every wall, Luc realized.

"He collected them. Some were specially ordered

from San Francisco. That was years ago. I remember how excited he'd get when a box would arrive.'' Dani smiled. ''Some he picked up at estate sales. And some his father bought after he'd emigrated here from Poland. He said his father always lamented the library he'd left behind, but he felt it was imperative that they get out of the country. His wife was Jewish, you see.''

Luc lifted first one, then another, loving the feel of the worn leather, the well-thumbed pages, the crinkle of the leaves. Occasionally, an inscription caught his eye and he would try to decipher the thin Spenserian letters on the flyleaf of a Jane Austen novel, or the boldly slashed signatures on more manly tomes.

''These are wonderful.'' He glanced up at her. ''I don't know how you can bear to sell them.''

''If I don't think about it, it's easier,'' Dani informed him quietly.

He could have kicked himself for the thoughtless remark, but she didn't give him a chance, rising and walking out the door toward the kitchen before he could think of a suitable response.

''Come on, we'd better check that pizza. I don't want it burned. I'm starved.''

Luc set the books aside and rose to follow.

The pizza was cooked to perfection, golden and steaming, loaded with everything he favored.

''I just remembered I was supposed to bring lunch.'' Luc stared at her. ''I forgot all about it. I guess I was nervous about riding.''

''It doesn't matter. I'll catch you next time.''

He allowed himself to smile. *Next time.* He would hold her to that.

''Do you want to eat in front of the fire?'' Dani

tugged a carton of grape juice from the fridge, poured two glasses and held one out.

He shook his head, adamant. "No way. Those books are too valuable. You shouldn't even have a fire in that room, let alone pizza and juice."

Dani shrugged, flopped down at the table and motioned him to do the same.

"Nothing's happened in all these years, I don't think it's going to happen now. But okay, the kitchen it is. I'll say grace." She murmured a quick thanks, then took a huge bite of her pizza and munched contentedly.

"Did your father have the books appraised and insured?" he asked, his curiosity growing. He'd known Dermot was well read, but who would have guessed the old philosophers were a favorite of that blustering man. Luc had counted three books on Plato, and he'd barely begun to examine the cache.

"Yes, he used to insure them." She nodded, her gaze fixed on the window as if she could see something out there that interested her. "Once, years ago, he had a fellow come out and appraise them. But I let the insurance go. It was simply costing too much. That's one reason why I'd like to sell them. Besides, I'd rather someone else enjoy them than have them sit on the shelves, getting dustier." She said it cheerfully, as if those gorgeous volumes meant nothing to her.

Luc couldn't understand that.

"But, Dani, don't you want to keep them? Doesn't it bother you?"

"Sometimes. If I let myself dwell on it. But only because my father loved them. A couple of the poets I'll keep for myself. They hold special memories of my mother…." Her voice dropped away. When she resumed speaking, the emotion was gone. "The rest are just things, Doc. They're nice, they're pretty, but I don't need them to live. If they fetch a few pennies, the bank will be more than happy to accept it as repayment on my debt.''

"But—'' He frowned, not knowing how to express his sadness that she was forced to part with this important piece of her heritage.

"It has to be done. Don't fuss, okay?''

He knew then that she had shed plenty of tears over her decision. But she wouldn't change her mind. She had such pluck, and a solid strength of character that belied her years.

"After you've had them appraised, may I be permitted to buy some? My grandfather was an avid reader and I have very fond memories of sitting at his feet, listening to Aesop's fables and so many other stories.''

"I'll make you a deal, Doc.'' Dani slipped another piece of pizza onto his plate, though he'd already eaten four.

"Thanks. It's very good.''

"Don't sound so surprised. Even I can't wreck frozen pizza. Except maybe by burning.'' She took another slice for herself, sipped some juice, then narrowed her gaze.

"Uh-oh. I don't like that look.''

"What look?'' She lifted her eyebrows, tried to feign innocence.

The futility of her gesture almost made Luc chuckle. She was such fun to be with. How long had it been since he'd had fun with anyone?

"Never mind pretending. Let's just say I know when you're up to something, and you, Dani DeWitt, are up to something. You'd better tell me what your offer of a deal means.''

"I'm not up to anything. What a distrustful thing to say." She lifted her plate and glass, tucked them into the dishwasher, then pranced out of the room.

Luc took his time finishing his own pizza, then followed. She was kneeling on the floor when he entered the study, her head bent as she squinted at the roman numerals on a tattered volume's flyleaf.

"What's wrong?"

"Look at this date and tell me what you see." She wiggled a little to make room for him among the books.

Luc looked. Then looked again. Finally he stared at Dani.

"Does that say what I think it does?" he murmured, as if to speak too loudly would change the date.

"I don't know. I get all mixed up with those letters. Let's see." She grabbed a sheet of notepaper and began to copy the letters. "Now the *M* stands for—"

"The date is 1648, Dani." He carefully lifted the volume from her hands and moved it to a secure place on a shelf far from the crackling fireplace. "It's very rare."

"I don't suppose it will be worth much since it's so badly tattered." She frowned in disgust.

"You might be surprised." He tried to control his excitement. "I worked in an emergency room in New York a while back. A friend took me to a big auction house for my birthday. They had some old books." He named the highest selling figure. "That was for a book that wasn't as old as this and in far worse condition."

"Really?" She clasped her hands in excitement. "Maybe I really can pay down that debt."

His beeper went off, drawing his attention away from the gorgeous woman with the sheen of pure excitement glittering from the depths of her eyes. His heart sunk as he read the message.

"It's Joshua. Can I use your phone?"

She nodded, and he placed the call, then answered Nicole's litany of questions.

"I'm at Dani's. We're looking at some old books her father had. Yes, I know how hard it's raining. Oh, I didn't think of that. I see. Well, I can try, but the road might slow me down. You would? Thank you, Nicole. I owe you big time."

He hung up, unable to hide his grin.

"I take it that was good news." Dani glanced up at him from her position on the floor.

"A case at the hospital. I forgot I'm supposed to be on call tonight after eight. Nicole's handling it for me."

"Good." She waited for him to sit down again, and when he didn't, she frowned. "Do you want to hear my deal or not?"

Deal? Oh yeah. She'd been planning something.

"Of course I want to hear it." He hoped.

"I'll give you riding lessons, provide the horse and show you the best trails around here, if you'll help me catalog these books. I purposely left it because I knew it would take forever, and because I was busy with the stock. But most of the cattle are gone now. If two of us did it together, it shouldn't take that long to list everything that's here."

He could tell from the look on her face that cataloging was not one of her favorite pastimes. But he wouldn't turn her down. No way. Turn down a chance to spend time with her out here in the place she loved best? Refuse a chance to handle books so rare that few people ever got to see them? He almost laughed out loud at the preposterousness of it.

Lucas Lawrence had never been called a fool.

Sure, Dani was a younger woman. She was ready to set out on the journey of her lifetime and he was ready to settle down. She needed to find out what life could offer her; he thought he already knew.

But maybe, for a few hours every so often, he could pretend he was young again, looking forward to the future. Who would it hurt? Dani didn't think of him as anything more than an actor in her play, a convenient friend she could call on. He'd made a point of telling her he wasn't looking for anything more than friendship, so she wouldn't think it was strange if he spent time with her, cataloging her father's library.

"Luc? Is it a deal?"

He nodded. "It's a deal," he agreed solemnly.

A few carefree hours spent with a girl who knew exactly what she wanted from life and went after it with a vengeance.

What was wrong with that?

Chapter Six

"**P**erfect! You are all excellent actors worthy of an Oscar." Dani couldn't quite stem the exuberance she felt and she didn't care how much it showed as she congratulated her team.

For the first time they'd run through the play from beginning to end without a hitch. Well, she wouldn't count Luc's stumbles, but even he had soon caught on to the idea of consulting his notebook whenever he forgot his lines and needed a reminder. Was he a little less nervous now? She definitely thought so.

"You know, I never really paid attention before, but this play has a lot of hidden meanings and nuances." Big Ed scratched his chin thoughtfully as he scanned the photocopied sheets. "I'd sure like to know who wrote it. Don't we have to have permission to perform it or something?"

Dani's heart did a quick two-step but she kept her face impassive.

"Don't worry, Ed, we have permission," she assured him, turning away to gather up her own notes.

"Yes, but usually the author's name is printed below the title." Millicent Maple, who played a little old busybody, was true to life as she flipped the photocopied sheets over, then back. "Far as I can see, there's no one's name on here."

"Really?" Dani pretended to examine her own pages. "I must have left it off when I copied it." She stuffed her copy of the play inside, closed her bag and slung it over one shoulder, then lifted her head. "Same time next week?" she asked, scanning her actors' faces.

They nodded. Only Luc remained silent, his brown eyes dark, his forehead furrowed as if he were considering something that puzzled him.

"Yes. Next week." They filed out of the fellowship hall one by one, until only she and Luc were left behind.

"We've only got two months left until the performances," he mused quietly. "Do you think we should start rehearsing in the camp building?"

Dani considered it, nodded. "Good idea, though it would be nice to have the props for that. It might be a chore to lug them back and forth. Summer's a busy time for everyone." She preceded him to the door. "Are you still planning on coming out to the ranch after church tomorrow?" she asked, trying not to sound too eager.

"I thought you'd probably forget or want to call it off." He grinned at her frown of confusion. "The Sunday-school picnic, remember? Right after the service. You are going?"

He waited while she locked the hall, then walked with her to her truck. The night was warm and still quite light, with stars just beginning to flicker overhead. The pungent aroma of freshly worked earth permeated the air, and she noticed that someone had already filled the church beds with a variety of bedding plants. Months had passed since her father's death. The hurt was still there, but Dani was learning to accept it, to deal with her life as it was.

"Well? Are you going or not?"

She blinked, tried to remember what they'd been discussing. Oh, the church picnic.

"Sure, I'll go. I still have the horses to look after, but I can do that in the morning and—"

"I really need you to come, Dani," he said, looking forlorn.

Dani stared. He *needed* her? She tried to read his expression and couldn't.

"You need me? Why?"

"I need your help, Dani. In fact, I'm desperate."

Desperate? For her help? She couldn't believe he'd said it.

It was true, their relationship had evolved into an easy camaraderie that made being with Luc relaxing and fun. She'd never known anyone like him. Luc didn't fuss about a mess, or worry if he measured up to someone else's standard. He had his own particular brand of integrity that went beyond the medical creed of "do no harm."

Perhaps he hadn't realized it himself yet, but Luc fit in around Blessing. She had watched him lately, especially during practice. He picked up the slack, took it upon himself to reach out to those whom others had forgotten, but he did it in such a quiet, unassuming way that the townsfolk seldom noticed.

He'd begun doing the same thing whenever he came to the ranch, offering to mow the grass or paint a fence. At first she'd thought he was trying to repay her for the riding lessons, but now she realized that pitching in was just part and parcel of who Luc was.

"What could you possibly need me for?" she wondered aloud.

He shuffled his feet against the sidewalk, turned his face out of the light so she couldn't read his eyes. But Dani knew those gestures well enough to be sure he was hiding something. She planted herself in front of him and stood, hands on her hips, waiting.

"You'd better tell me, Luc."

He frowned, shoved his hands into his pockets and sighed.

"Joshua and Nicole have elected me to handle the kids' games for the picnic."

Dani blinked. "You? Why you, pray tell? What do you know about kids?"

He harrumphed his disgust.

"Quite a lot, as it happens. I am a doctor, after all."

She nodded. "Who *treats* children. You don't play with them. I've never even seen you playing with the Darling girls, and they're as sweet as buttons."

"Which only goes to show what you know." He edged his way around her and continued walking down the street, obviously unaware that he'd passed her truck. "I've baby-sat them several times, actually. Last week I was over for dinner."

"I know. You told me." What on earth could have caused that sour look?

"Not all of it, I didn't." He glanced over his shoulder as if he suspected someone of listening in, then began whispering. "They tied me up."

"What?" She stared at him. "What are you talking about, Luc? And stop that silly whispering. The Darling girls are long since asleep."

"Ha! I'm beginning to wonder if they ever sleep." He raked one hand through his already tousled hair.

"They wanted me to talk about the ranch, so I made up this stupid story about lassoing cattle and stuff. Then they wanted to play a game. Somehow it ended up with me getting trussed up like a turkey."

A mental picture of Luc's dilemma made Dani double over with laughter. "Which one suggested that?" she burbled, then held up a hand. "Never mind, I don't think I want to know."

"The point is," he said, "that I am in no way qualified to handle a bunch of kids, especially when it comes to organizing games for them. I need help."

He was serious. Sympathy wiggled its way into her heart, but she resisted.

"You said you looked after your siblings. Surely you must have played a game or two with them."

He shrugged. "Sure. Baseball, basketball. But they weren't that young. They didn't need me to organize their games." He checked his watch, made a face. "Look, we're wasting time. Will you help me or not?"

He'd helped her catalog, then pack up her father's books, even driven with her into Denver to meet the seller. He hadn't complained, hadn't told her how disorganized she was. He'd just *been there*. It was time she repaid him.

"Relax, I'll help. You can buy me lunch while we discuss strategies."

Four hours later, as they cleaned up the remains of balloons blown apart during a popping game Dani had devised, Luc figured they'd be asking him to do this again next year. Success didn't begin to cover the kids' enthusiasm this afternoon.

Wait a minute—*next year?* Would he even be here next year?

"If I'd known you were so good at entertaining, Nicole and I would have asked you to watch the girls before." Joshua Darling stood five feet away, arms akimbo, eyes twinkling with fun. "Your games were the hit of the whole picnic."

"Hey, maybe he should consider renting himself out for birthday parties." Gray pulled out his wallet. "Cody's got one coming up in the fall. How much would it cost me to have you take over the whole thing?"

"What a good idea, boys. And of course there's the Christmas party. We always need someone to handle the games there." Miss Winifred stood behind Gray, grinning. "I do believe you could make a good living, Luc. That is, if you're staying?"

He frowned, scanned her face and found the telltale glimmer in her eyes that told him she was up to something.

"What do you mean, if?" Gray accepted his young son from his wife, then swung the boy up to perch on his shoulders. Cody giggled in delight.

Luc clutched the garbage bag he was using a little tighter, conscious of all eyes on him. At the edge of the group Dani stood as if frozen in place, her green eyes swirling with emotion. He couldn't seem to look away from them.

"I never said I wasn't leaving," he said slowly.

Her voice was soft, condemning. "You never said you were."

"You can't leave now." Joshua's insistent declaration drew everyone's stare. "I mean—"

"What he means is that we're going to have a baby." Nicole looped her arm through her husband's, gazed up at him adoringly. After a moment, she turned to Luc.

"We're going to need a partner, Lucas. Someone who can fill in for me in seven months, while I take some time off to get to know my baby."

The rush of congratulations saved Luc from having to answer the questions he saw on Dani's face, and knew she wondered why he hadn't accepted. He didn't know how to explain nor what he could say the next time someone asked about his future. Who would understand that something held him back from making a commitment. The Darlings had approached him before about the possibility of a partnership and he'd put them off. How much longer could he do that and stay in Blessing, enjoy the camaraderie he'd found here?

He watched Dani congratulate the couple while his mind dispassionately sorted through the facts. Nicole's pregnancy meant they'd be looking for a permanent solution in the office, and if he wasn't going to accept their offer, someone else would. If they found their partner, he would be redundant, both in the practice and in Blessing. He would have to leave.

He glanced around, searching for Dani. But she'd disappeared. His heart sank to his toes. Then he realized the others were staring at him curiously.

"Congratulations, both of you." Conscious of the length of time that had elapsed between their announcement and his response, he tried to make a joke out of it. "I would have said that earlier, but I was in shock." He hugged Nicole, shook Joshua's hand. "Are you hoping for a boy or a girl?"

"A healthy baby is all we're praying for. The rest is up to God."

"As it should be." Miss Winifred's huge smile could scarcely fit upon her face. "You've reminded me of something I read just this morning. It was written by

Helen Mellincost. A man was regretting the past and fearing the future. Suddenly God spoke. 'My name is I am.' He waited and God spoke again. 'When you live in the past, with its mistakes and regrets, it is hard. I am not there. My name is not I was. When you live in the future, with its problems and fears, it is hard. I am not there. My name is not I will be. When you live in this moment, it is not hard. I am here. My name is I am.' ''

Her glance fell on him, and Luc shifted under the scrutiny, knowing very well that the little homily was meant especially for him.

''That's a good thing to remember, Aunt Win. Well, we need to get three very dirty girls home and into the tub. Thanks again, Luc. Let us know as soon as you decide.'' Joshua slipped his hand into his wife's and they strolled across the grass. After a moment, their daughters clustered around them, chattering a mile a minute.

''We have to go too. Adam's supposed to stop by.'' Gray's face contorted into a grimace. ''I was afraid to ask what he wanted.''

''What he *needs* is a wake-up call,'' Marissa mumbled. She smiled apologetically, her glance shifting to Miss Winifred. ''Adam is trying to convince himself that Gray is pretending to be Harris McGonigle's son so he can cheat Adam out of his birthright. His constant complaints are wearing a little thin.''

''Keep praying. Goodbye, Cody.'' Winifred reached up and tickled the boy under his chin. ''Next time your mom and dad bring you into town, you stop and see me. I've got a special treat for you.''

''Thanks.'' Cody wiggled to get a look at his father's face. ''Can we go today, Dad?''

Gray laughed, tossed him in the air. "The bakery isn't open today, buddy. But we'll go soon. I promise."

As Marissa threaded her arm through her husband's, Gray's steady glance met Luc's.

"This is a no-brainer, Doc," he said. "God sent you to Blessing, we need you here and you want to stay. For several reasons." He winked. "All you have to do is say the word."

"See you." Luc deliberately ignored his advice.

"See you, Luc. And thanks." Marissa stood on tiptoe, brushed her lips against his cheek. "I know you're sick of advice," she whispered. "So I won't give you any. I'll just tell you what I've been thinking. Okay?"

He shrugged. "Can I stop you?"

She giggled. "No. Okay, here's what I think." She paused for effect, then said, "Just because a doctor finds a name for a condition doesn't mean he knows what it is."

"You're starting to sound like Miss Winifred." With an apologetic bow to that lady, he turned back to Marissa. "I suppose you're implying something along the lines of 'physician, heal thyself'?"

"I always said you'd be a quick study if you set your mind to it." Gray slapped him on the shoulder, then turned and raced Cody across the grass. Marissa followed more sedately.

"Feel like sharing some French onion soup?"

Jolted from his introspection, Luc twisted, saw the baker still waiting for him.

"That's very kind of you, Miss Win. But after this afternoon, I think I'd just like to find a quiet spot and unwind. I'm a little old for that many kids all at once."

"Age is a matter of the mind. If you think you're too old, you'll soon feel too old. On the other hand, if you grasp life with both hands and squeeze out every bit of enjoyment you can, you will never grow old.''

More advice. And it was probably good advice, but he couldn't forget that look of shock and hurt he'd seen on Dani's face.

"Luc?'' Miss Winifred's soft white hand touched his arm. "Is everything all right? Can I help?''

"Everything is fine,'' he told her, drawing himself erect as he repelled the urge to expose his feelings. "I just haven't made a decision about staying.''

"Why is that?'' The clear blue of her gaze poked straight through his pretense to the heart of him.

"It's a nice town. I like the people a lot. I enjoy the work. Nicole and Joshua have been wonderful.''

"But?''

"There are a lot of things for me to think about.'' Persistence didn't begin to describe Winifred.

"Such as?''

He sighed, mentally organizing his argument.

"The investment, for one thing. I've already got substantial debts from medical school. The permanence. The distance from my family.''

"I'm sure the Darlings are more than willing to accommodate your financial needs. And permanence isn't a reason to leave, it's a reason to stay. Besides, if you decided you didn't like it, you could always sell out to a new partner.'' She ticked the reasons off on her fingers. "As for your family, how is it that their distance never seemed to bother you before? You told me your sister doesn't live near your two brothers.''

"She doesn't, but—'' Rat-a-tat-tat. The words kept pinging off him. Frustration gnawed inside. Why couldn't they just let him be? It wasn't as if he was going to run away tomorrow.

"What's really at the root of your indecisiveness, Luc?"

"I'm not being indecisive. All I'm asking for is some time to consider all the angles of a choice like this. It's a big commitment, one I don't want to make and then regret."

Winifred Blessing wrapped an arm around his shoulders. "You'll forgive my meddling, won't you, dear? Because you know I only want what is best for you and I can see how much you're struggling with this."

He sighed. She'd tell him anyway—he might as well be polite and listen to another hunk of unasked-for advice.

"Go ahead."

"Your problem has nothing to do with commitment, Luc."

He reared back, frowning at her. "How can you say that? Of course it has. I'm trying to plot the course of my life for the next forty or so years."

She shook her head. "You don't have that power, son. Only God controls the future."

"I know that."

"Do you?" She offered him a tiny smile. "You and Dani, you're so alike, each trying to manage your world to maximum advantage. Each afraid to let go and surrender the controls to the One who loves you more than you can even imagine."

"Surrender?" The word snagged in his brain.

"Surrender means you go one step beyond belief—that you forget yourself and your pride, all the things that stand in the way—"

"Stand in the way of what?" he interrupted, a tinge of anger curling inside. "I'm trying to do the right thing. I'm trying to make a responsible decision. Is that wrong?''

She nodded.

"Why?"

''Because you're using yourself and your feelings and your doubts as the meter by which you gauge this decision. You're depending on yourself, your intellect, your past experiences, your pride. You're trying to control something that's beyond your control.'' She shook her head. ''It won't work, Lucas. God brought you here at exactly the right time with exactly the gifts this town needed. All He's asking now is that you surrender your doubts, and let Him show you the next step to a fuller life.''

Surrender. That word again.

''But what if it's the wrong step? What if I make a colossal mistake?''

''Is God too small to handle that? Couldn't He direct you away from Blessing if it wasn't His will for you to be here?'' Winifred's voice dropped as a group of people walked past. But her words were no less powerful. ''Follow your heart, Luc. That nudging inside you that tells you this decision is too big for you, that's God telling you He has a plan. Not your plan. His plan. And you're going to have to trust Him to let it unfold.''

''But the commitment—''

She placed her hands on her hips and glared at him. ''Did you stop and think about the *commitment* you'd be making when you took over raising your family? Did you consider the *commitment* you'd have to make to finish medical school, to pay the bills, to put food on the table?''

''Well, no, but—''

She laughed. ''Don't feed me this *commitment* babble

any longer, Lucas Lawrence. Face the truth. You're running scared. Now would be a good time to give up and let God handle things. He's a lot better at it than you are.''

Having said her piece, the town matriarch marched across the park grass, and set off down the street, her sneaker heels striking the cement in a steady tap-tap rhythm.

Surrender.

He dumped the trash bag into the nearest container, checked that the area was now clear of debris, then headed for home.

Surrender what?

You depend on yourself. Depend on God.

Surely if God wanted him to stay in Blessing, he'd feel at peace about it…wouldn't he?

Luc spent the rest of the afternoon and well into the evening sitting on his back porch contemplating his life, tossing and turning the decision of a future in Blessing to look at first one side, then the other.

When he could tolerate the internal battle no longer, he decided to go for a walk. Perhaps he could clear his mind. He locked the front door, then started down the stairs, almost missing the square white box that sat to one side of the door.

''Oh no. Not again.'' He picked it up, lifted the lid and, with growing apprehension, scanned the contents.

Sure enough, a fat, white, heart-shaped cookie lay inside with a message written in red.

A ship is safer in harbor, but it's not meant for that.

Luc lifted the cookie from the box, letting the cardboard drop to the porch. He glared at it for a moment, then took a huge bite. The buttery treat melted on his tongue as he jumped off the stairs and started down the sidewalk.

"I get it, okay. I get it." He crunched the words into oblivion.

Surrender. Trust.

Easy to say. Quite different to put into action.

Chapter Seven

Dani hunkered over Duke's neck and surveyed the shimmering landscape before her. July Fourth had arrived in a rush of blistering heat that not even the mountain breezes could cool today.

"Where do you want to ride this time?" she asked, glancing at Luc's sober face.

"Anywhere. I just want to get my mind off of work."

"I'm sorry about Mrs. Murphy," she offered.

"So am I. She was my first patient when I came to Blessing. It's hard to realize she's gone." He turned his head away, scanned the lush green stands of spruce and pine at the foot of the nearest mountain, and pointed. "Man, it's hot out here. How come we never ride in there? It's got to be cooler in the shade."

"It takes a little more skill to ride among trees," Dani warned. "The boughs are low and they sting if you forget to duck."

"Are you saying I'm not up to it?" He thought he'd been doing pretty well this past month.

"It's tougher riding, Luc. Are you sure you're not

too tired? You must have had a long night, waiting in case the family needed you.''

He hadn't told her that. How had she known he'd hung around the corridors, crept into the room from time to time, wanting to be there in case there was something he could do? Of course, there had been nothing. Mrs. Murphy's cancer had progressed too far.

''I am tired,'' he admitted, ''but it's not that kind of tired. I'll be fine.''

He held her stare, his own expression dark and brooding, the glints of fun she'd come to expect now dampened. Dani considered the risks of allowing a novice to ride in the woods where a squirrel or rabbit could cause complications. But she decided the forced concentration would take his mind off the death of poor Mrs. Murphy, and the young family she'd left behind.

''Come on, then. But be careful.'' She let Duke have his head, using her knee occasionally to urge him around a boulder, but returning always to the almost overgrown path. ''You know, I haven't been here in ages. Dad used to love it in here in the summer.''

''I can see why.'' Luc gazed at the thick green canopy overhead and smiled. ''It's at least ten degrees cooler and it smells fresh and clean.''

''Not exactly a farm person, are you,'' Dani teased. ''How can a doctor be so squeamish about things like snails?''

''I'm not squeamish.''

He didn't offer the usual banter, didn't even comment when the path narrowed so that he had to follow behind her. When she turned to find what kept him silent, Dani saw his gaze moving among the trees.

''It's like another world,'' he said. ''As if we dropped

through Alice's looking glass to a whole different place. Look at the size of those ferns!''

She said nothing, hoping he'd absorb the same peace and tranquility her father had found here. He'd always maintained that the solitude of his own private forest had prompted him to build...

The cabin!

"I'd forgotten about that." She realized she'd inadvertently stopped Duke.

"Forgotten what?" Luc rode beside her now through an open grassy section.

"The cabin. It's been ages since I was there. I don't even know if it's still standing. Actually, I'm not even sure I can find it anymore." Suddenly it seemed imperative that she make an effort to locate the old stone building, as a kind of farewell to her father and the things he'd loved about the ranch.

"There's a cabin in here?" Luc surveyed the rugged, untouched land. "Where?"

"It's a bit of a ride in. If you don't think you can handle it, I can come another day." But oh, she wanted to go today.

"I can handle it." As if to prove it, Luc jogged along beside her for several moments without speaking. But his curiosity couldn't be contained. "How could he build in here? It would be pretty tough to carry lumber through this, and he'd have to hand saw everything."

"He didn't use lumber, he used stones. River rock. And yes, what trees he felled, he had to do it all by hand. Most of the actual building was done before my time, but I remember when he was finishing it. I was about four or five and I'd play by the river while he worked. He built a kind of corral in the water to fence me in. I paddled around there for hours, catching minnows or blowing bubbles. When he got hot, he'd jump in and teach me to swim. At night we'd have a fire. Sometimes we even camped out here.''

"Sounds like heaven."

"I thought it was," she murmured. Heaven's kiss, she mused. Was this where the idea had come from?

They rode silently after that, single file through the dense brush, then side by side when it opened up here and there. Eventually they emerged into a meadow where wildflowers tossed their pretty heads in the light breeze that danced across the valley and over the water. For a moment it was enough just to sit and look, and remember.

"This is fantastic."

Luc's soft whisper of admiration touched Dani deeply. At least they shared something in common.

"There's the cabin. It doesn't look too bad."

She nudged Duke to pick up the pace, and ten minutes later they arrived beside the stone cottage that looked as if it had been transplanted from some English dell.

"No wonder you want to keep this place. It's a treasure." Luc sat in his saddle, hands resting on the horn, and stared at her. "I hereby take back any stupid advice I've ever given suggesting you let the ranch go."

She smiled. "It's okay, Luc. How could you know that this is just one of so many special places?"

His eyes met hers. "I know you. I should have known."

A rush of tenderness welled inside at his softly spoken words. Perhaps he did understand.

"Look, Dani," he whispered, reaching out to touch her hand. His fingers just naturally threaded through hers. "Look at that."

Dani forced her concentration off the rush of feeling his touch evoked and onto the scene in front of her. A deer and her two fawns grazed on the lush green grass that grew in a strip between cabin and river. The doe paused, raised her head and sniffed the wind when Duke snorted his desire to be free. A moment later she bounded across the open space, her babies following as nimbly as they could. The three disappeared into the trees that protected the little stone house from the mountains behind.

"That was your welcoming committee," Dani told him, amused by the stunned surprise on his face.

"Thank you. I appreciate it." The dark glint was back in his eyes as his hand slipped from hers. He patted Flower to calm her, then glanced around, sniffed the wind. "Smells like someone's having a campfire."

She chuckled, shook her head. "The welcoming party isn't that efficient, I'm afraid. It's probably something Gray's burning. He owns the land next to this, remember. His starts about four miles over. His father and mine had an agreement to leave this section of the land untouched."

"Obviously two very forward-thinking men." He followed her lead, reining Flower to a halt as they approached the cabin. "A well?" he asked, eyes curious.

She smiled at the memories. "My father always said he didn't want to drink from the same source as the animals. He had a thing about that, so he dug the well. It's only about four feet deep and probably dry by now."

"It suits the place."

They dismounted, tethered the horses to nearby aspens.

"Why do you tie them now?"

Dani glanced at him, wondering how much to say, and eventually decided to tell the truth. "Sometimes there are cougars here. We have quite a way to go back and it's not very good walking."

"I see." He scanned the foothills but apparently decided all was safe for now. "Are you going inside?"

She nodded. "Might as well. I'd like to see how the old place has fared."

"The roof looks pretty good. I'm assuming he had to bring that in along with the windows?" Luc waited for her nod, then grazed his fingers over the rounded edges of the walls of river rock that Dermot had plastered together with some kind of clay. "The walls are in great condition."

"It was built to last." She unlatched the door, peered inside first, then let it swing wide. "It actually looks pretty good in here, especially since I haven't been here in ages."

Luc moved to stand beside her. "Good? It looks like you were here yesterday. There's no dust on anything."

"Well, there's not a lot of dust out here." But it was strange that nothing had blown in the doors or windows. Dani shrugged, moved around the room, on guard in case a mouse or squirrel dashed toward the door. But there was no evidence of animals.

The stone walls were free of cobwebs, though a layer of dust covered the windows. Luc wiped his sleeve across the mantel over the fireplace, then moved to the furniture.

"Hey, this is cool." He plopped down in a willow rocker. "It's really comfortable."

"Dad told me my mother made the furniture. She learned how to weave, and the willows around here provided her with lots of material." Dani's glance moved back to the fireplace. "I didn't realize he had books here." She slid her hands over the leather spines. "These aren't that old, not like those others. And look, they all seem to be the same."

She pulled one out and let it fall open. To her surprise, her father's writing scrawled across the page. She squealed at the sight of the date.

"Look at this, Luc."

He rose and walked over to her. "What is it?"

"A diary. My dad's." She carried it with her to the nearest chair, flopped down and began reading. "This is from before my mother died. When they were first married. They found this place together."

Dani scanned page after page as the memories poured out, bits and pieces of a life her father had sometimes described during long, blizzard-white days when no one ventured outside.

"Dani?"

She didn't know how much later it was that Luc's hand on her shoulder roused her from the book.

"It's getting late. I think we should head back."

She glanced at her watch, shocked to see that it was now after supper.

"I'm sorry, Luc. I didn't mean to abandon you. I just got caught up in this. It's a good thing it's summer and the sun hangs around a little longer or we'd have to camp here." She closed the book reluctantly. "But you're right. We should head home now."

She walked to the shelf, prepared to put the diary back. But she couldn't. She wanted to read it, read all of them and follow her father's life through the years. The things that were important to him were in these diaries. These books would be part of the history she would always keep.

"Luc, do you think you can handle an extra pack on your saddle?"

"I guess. Why? What are you thinking?"

"I'm thinking it would be a shame to leave these books here for something to ruin. I want to take them back with me." She walked toward the old table her father had planed by hand from a massive spruce tree. "He used to leave…ah, I thought so." She triumphantly showed off her prize—two gunnysacks. "We'll use these to carry them."

He helped her pack the twelve fat books, six in each sack, then scrounged out a piece of twine and tied one sack to each saddle.

"If you had supplies, a person could manage out here quite nicely," Luc noted, studying the battered old pots that hung on the wall, the three cups and plates that sat on the table. There was even a can of beans in the cupboard. A coal-oil lamp swung from the roof, and he checked the fluid.

"Enough to last quite a while," he told her.

"Tell you what, you bone up on your riding skills and I'll rent you the place for a weekend. The exorbitant prices those back-to-nature people charge to spend out in the wilderness will help me with the mortgage." She grinned at his snort of disgust, secured the latch on the door, then double-checked that nothing could push its way inside.

"I thought the mortgage thing was better." Luc stared at the almost overgrown path leading up the hill. "Where does that lead?"

Dani stifled a grin. "My memories are a little hazy," she told him. "But if I recall, that leads to the facilities."

"Oh."

"Not as interested now?" she teased, and vaulted into her seat. "Rustic always looks nice from a distance, but when it gets down to the nitty-gritty, I do like my hot shower."

But Luc wasn't listening. He'd shifted his position on Flower so that he was facing the cabin and its idyllic setting.

"You could swim in the lake," he suggested. "There's even a canoe over there."

"I doubt it's usable. C'mon, Luc. Let's go before you try and talk me into a camp-out. I didn't bring any bug repellent, and the mosquitoes from years ago left an indelible impression."

He followed her away from the meadow and the cabin, pausing only once to glance back. Dani could think of nothing to say, and Luc didn't seem inclined to talk. They rode in silence.

By the time they arrived at Dani's, the horses were clearly tired. Dani was too, but knew she couldn't rest until they were fed and watered.

Luc worked alongside her, in a quiet companionship that seemed as natural as it was welcome.

"I'm beginning to really enjoy riding," he told her, watching as she scooped out some oats for each horse. "I don't ache nearly as much and I find it easier to look around and admire the scenery."

"Good. Soon you and Flower will be moving as one." She patted the graceful slope of each horse's neck, then clicked off the stable lights. "Come on, I'll see if I can find us a cold drink."

"Thanks."

The sun had begun its descent in a fiery ball of red that lent a pink glow to the horizon. Luc wanted to watch it from the porch, so Dani carried out two glasses of juice.

"I turned on the grill," she told him, sinking into her favorite chair. "It doesn't seem quite right that you should have brought steaks out to a ranch, but I'm so hungry, I won't argue."

"Good. I was given them anyway, so it's not as if I'm breaking some rule. I just hope that cooler did its job." He sat down beside her. "Thanks," he murmured, his hand finding hers. His palm covered it, warming her skin with his.

"For what?"

"For letting me regroup without asking a lot of questions. For showing me your father's special place. For just being here." He leaned forward and brushed her lips with his. "I really appreciate your friendship, Dani."

She blinked. Kissing was part of their friendship now?

"Aren't you going to say anything?" The familiar crooked smile was back. "Are you mad?"

"Why would I be mad?"

"I don't know. But I've never seen you at a loss for words before. Was it the kiss? Did I offend you?"

Dani grappled to find the right response. Perhaps if the world stopped spinning for a minute she could figure out how to deal with this rush of crazy, mixed-up feelings.

What on earth was going on with Dr. Lucas Lawrence? Hadn't he said, mere weeks ago, that he was only interested in friendship? Had something changed and he'd forgotten to tell her?

"Tell me what you're feeling."

"Confusion." The word spilled out. Dani peered at

him. "I thought you said—" She stopped. There was no way to phrase this delicately.

His arm slid around her shoulders and he snuggled her against his side.

"I guess I need to explain," he said.

"Go ahead." She wished someone would explain why it felt perfectly natural to sit on this bench beside him. She waited, only half her attention on the gorgeous sunset.

Luc said nothing for a long time, but eventually his voice emerged, quiet, reflective.

"As you so concisely pointed out—several times, I might add—I've been sort of holding back when it came to getting involved in Blessing. Most of the things I've done have been because someone conscripted me."

"Okay."

He smiled at her guarded response.

"I can hear the wheels grinding. The next question you have is why have I done that."

She waited.

"I'm afraid I don't have a very good answer for you, Dani. But the gist of it is that I've been...sort of waiting."

"Waiting for what?"

"That's the hard part." He scratched his neck, peering out into the evening light. "I had this idea that if I waited until all the data were in, all the information was collected in my brain, I could rationally sort through it and decide whether or not my future is here." He twisted to look at her, his face serious. "What I was trying to do was to avoid making a mistake, avoid having to start over."

"That's important to you—not starting over?" For the first time, Dani felt as if she could see into Luc's brain, catch a glimpse of his soul. It was a disquieting sensation, and she returned her stare to the yard. Dust motes danced in the red haze from the sun so that the very air seemed to shimmer with an unearthly glow.

"I've started over so many times, you can't imagine. When my parents died, when my grandparents died, when I quit school, when I returned to school. Every time I took another temporary job I knew I'd be starting over when it was done."

His hand tightened on her shoulder, though Dani doubted he realized it. He was intent on explaining, his body still, his face mere inches from hers.

"I thought Blessing would be the same. I expected to do my job, pick up and get out of there after a few months. I wasn't really prepared to consider it as home. When you suggested it, well—" He shrugged. "It made me nervous, I suppose."

"Why?"

Silence stretched between them, but she said nothing, sensing that he needed a moment to organize what was in his mind so that he could explain.

"Why am I nervous?" He sighed. "Because maybe I'm not good at staying in one place. Maybe I've been temporary so long, I don't know how to be permanent." The words seemed to burst from him.

She stared into his eyes and saw the swirl of emotions clouding their depths and waited.

"The truth is, settling down in one place scares me."

Strong, competent Luc was scared? Dani could hardly believe what he was saying, but the proof was written all over his face. He shifted and patted her shoulder before he removed his arm to lean both elbows on his knees and stare at his feet.

"Luc, this makes no sense. Why should you be afraid

of building a life in Blessing?'' She nudged him in the ribs. ''Look at me. What's behind this?''

''Miss Winifred thinks I'm trying to control things instead of leaving my life up to God.''

Dani considered that. ''It makes sense. If you keep moving, God never gets a chance to show you what He can do.''

''I—I guess.''

''There's more to it than that, though.'' She thought about her own past, her fears, the things that ate at her. Who was she to advise anyone? She whispered a prayer for guidance.

''I think it has to do with your childhood,'' she blurted. ''With the way your parents left you. Luc, tell me about them.''

He didn't look at her. ''I don't remember much. They were gone a lot. They'd come home for holidays, breaks between trips. We'd move back home, settle in, then they'd be off again.''

''Turning your life upside down each time.'' Compassion rose inside her. ''Luc, did you resent your parents for leaving you?''

''I understood they had a job to do, that they needed to go.''

''That's not what I asked.''

He straightened, glared at her. ''All right. Yes, I hated it that my grandparents wore themselves out looking after us instead of retiring to someplace warm and enjoying life while my parents cavorted around Europe, staying in nice hotels, seeing all the sights. I detested moving back and forth every time they decided to come home. But I understood. That was their job.''

''Understanding doesn't make it any easier. You felt uprooted, a perfectly normal reaction for a child in those circumstances. And later you had to uproot your siblings to find work, didn't you?'' She nodded, not needing his agreement. ''Maybe more than once. Don't you see? You didn't do it on purpose, Luc. It was a means to an end, a way to pay the bills and give them their dreams. You did it, and you did very well. But, Luc, that's over. Now it's time to think about what you want for the rest of your life.''

He glanced over one shoulder, his eyes narrowed.

''What do you think I want, Dani?''

''I think you know. You're just trying to decide if you deserve it.'' She got up, put a hand on his shoulder. ''I'm going to put the steaks on. Stay here and think about what you see yourself doing in five years. Close your eyes and visualize it.''

She deliberately left him alone while she prepared baked potatoes, cut up a few carrot sticks and sliced some tomatoes. When the steaks were finished, she carried everything to the table on the porch. Luc was standing at the railing, peering into a dusky sky that never completely darkened during summer's short nights.

''Come and eat,'' she said.

He didn't move, and for a moment she didn't think he'd heard. Then he began to speak.

''Seeing that cabin today made me realize some things about myself,'' he told her. He stood with his back to her, staring at the horizon. ''There was so much peace, a sweet serenity there, at your father's hideout. I found myself thinking about living in such simple conditions, letting go of all the things that seem so necessary and just enjoying life.'' He sighed, then turned, moved toward the table. ''That's quite a legacy your father left you, Dani.''

Once he was seated, Dani poured two glasses of juice.

"You have a legacy, too, Luc. It's different than mine, I agree. But it's every bit as valuable. From what you've told me of your grandfather, he left you the legacy of compassion, of caring about other people, of giving above and beyond the call of duty. I think you're living up to that legacy just fine."

"Thanks."

They talked about other things then, and it was friendly conversation, light and not in the least introspective. But by the time they'd washed and dried the dishes, after Luc had helped her unpack the diaries, when the moon floated over the horizon, they both knew something had grown between them.

Dani walked him out to his car, waited while he fished out his keys.

"You asked me earlier to visualize my future. Do you want to know what I see?"

"Sure."

He reached out and, with one finger, tilted up her chin. "I see myself old, gray haired, living in a place that could be Blessing, enduring snowstorms and heat waves. I see people coming and going through my life, some I can help, some I can't."

She didn't know how to respond. Something in his voice kept her gaze riveted on him, so she wasn't surprised when he drew her into his arms.

"But today I saw something else. In every picture I imagined, I saw you, Dani. Laughing, teasing, daring me to race through town." He angled his head and brushed his lips across hers. "I'm years older than you. I've rambled all over the place. To think that, maybe,

Blessing could be home—it seems too good to be true. More than I deserve.''

She relished the words, felt them sink through to her soul…until his next sentence.

''I've been running away from the truth, Dani. But I don't think I can do that anymore. I want to build on this friendship. As long as I'm telling the truth, I might as well tell all of it.''

He paused, stared into her eyes, his own black pools telling her nothing.

''I think I want to be more than your friend. Is that going to be a problem?''

''I don't know.''

''At least you're honest.'' He tilted his head, drew her body to meet him.

Dani savored his kiss, allowed herself to melt into his arms and experience a range of emotions that were new and a little scary. But the primary feeling bubbling up inside was delight.

Still, she had to tell the whole truth. She couldn't lie or pretend she didn't have doubts about him. She tugged back an inch or so.

''I'm not sure I can be what you want, Luc,'' she whispered. ''I don't know if I can ever share those things with you. I let myself care too deeply once and it's taking a long time for me to get past that.''

''It hurt so much because he betrayed your trust.'' He nodded. ''I understand how devastating that can be. But I won't ever do that, Dani. I won't promise things I can't give you, I won't pretend to feel something I don't. And I won't ever take anything you don't want to give. I'm not him, Dani. The only thing I care about is you. You can trust me. I won't betray your trust.'' His arms coaxed her closer until his lips brushed her ear. "After all, I haven't told anyone you wrote that play, have I?"

She jerked back, stared at him. He knew?

"I found some of your college plays when we were cataloging those books. It wasn't hard to see your style in the one we're performing. You're very good, which is probably why the creep stole from you."

She frowned at that, but Luc continued.

"We'll go slow, let this friendship build into whatever God wants for us. I promise I won't push you into anything. I'll be happy just being with you."

She tried to think it through, to organize what he was saying into nice, neat lines. But it was too new, too—

"Don't leave me hanging here, please, Dani—"

His agonized voice drew her out of her reverie.

"If you think I'm too old for you, if you want to forget I ever said a word, just say so. I can handle it."

She laid her forefinger against his lips. "For now, let's just continue being friends and see what happens," she said softly, weaving her free hand into the longish curls that clung to his neck, and edging closer.

"I can tell you what happens," he whispered, snuggling her closer into his arms as he brushed a featherlight touch of his lips against her hair. "What happens is this—" He tilted his head lower until his mouth met hers.

"Nothing wrong with this," she murmured, wrapping her arms around his neck as she kissed him back.

"That's what I think—"

His beeper shot them both back to reality.

Groaning, Luc pulled his arm from her waist, yanked out the little box and checked the message.

"Mrs. Samson's in labor," he exclaimed. "I've got

to go. She threatened to sue me if I missed delivering her baby.''

''Then, you'd better go. Angie doesn't have long labors.'' She stepped away from him. ''Good night, Luc.''

''Dani, I—''

The beeper gave a second summons. He glared at it, then rolled his eyes.

''At least now you know what it's like to hang out with a doctor. Seems another delivery is imminent in Blessing. They sure know how to time them.''

They stared at each other, their glances conveying messages which required no words.

The beeper sounded a third time.

''Thanks. For everything.'' Luc drew her forward and planted a kiss on her lips, then climbed into his car and raced down the drive.

Dani stood for a moment, one hand touching her lips. Maybe heaven's kiss wasn't so far away when a man she cared about a lot had the same feelings for her. With her financial problems almost taken care of, she felt free, ready to embrace change, even ready to trust again.

She turned and walked into the house. She intended to lie in bed and contemplate what had just happened, but then she caught sight of her father's diaries. It wouldn't take long to read just one.

The night grew older, the moon rose to its zenith, then began a slow downward descent, but Dani barely noticed. Her attention was riveted on the words she read, then reread, unable to believe the evidence of her own eyes.

Years ago, Dermot had borrowed money from Harris McGonigle, Gray's father, to purchase the land where the cabin sat. But no matter how closely Dani read, no matter how many times she went back and forth, scanning the rounded handwriting, she could see no evidence this loan had ever been paid off.

Her heart quivered, then dipped to her toes as she pored over the old books. She continued reading until she arrived at the few remaining entries made in the days before Dermot's death. No mention was ever made of repayment. In fact, the only payment on record seemed to be in the gift of a horse that Dermot gave to Harris, a horse Dani had never heard of—Fancy Dancer.

Surely her father hadn't expected one horse, even a purebred one from his own breeding line, to cover the cost of the land?

At 4:00 a.m. the mantel clock chimed, forcing Dani out of her stupor of disbelief.

Betrayal burned deep in her heart. How could he do it? How could he have taken land and never paid for it? This was far worse than the bank bills she'd almost paid off. She scribbled calculations all over a yellow pad, heart sinking as the total appeared at the bottom. Twice, three times she calculated. The answer was the same.

Dani owed Grayson McGonigle a huge sum of money, plus thirty-two years' interest, and she had no possible means to repay it.

Unless she could find something to contradict Dermot's words, the ranch, the legacy Luc seemed so thrilled with, the one thing Dani had worked so hard to save, was not even hers.

Chapter Eight

"Okay, folks. Barely three weeks until play day. Let's nail this rehearsal, shall we?"

From stage left, Luc watched Dani summon a smile as she patiently waited for everyone to find their places. He remained offstage until she'd read the introduction, then ambled across the stage, and the play began. For now he'd have to concentrate, but as soon as he was finished, Luc intended to find out what was wrong.

Because there was something. She hadn't answered the phone for three days straight, and when she'd finally answered first thing this morning, she'd brushed him off. Was Dani climbing back into her protective shell?

He smiled wryly. Dani DeWitt was at once utterly mesmerizing and completely exasperating, but that didn't mean he was backing off. Not yet, anyway. He couldn't leave her alone.

Minus the interruptions that would happen on the nights of the actual presentation when the meal would be served in several courses, the entire play took less than an hour. Once the props had been stored, he forced himself to wait until Dani was free, scarcely paying attention to the other actors or the chitchat buzzing around him as he waited for an opening. He had to know if he'd blown it with her.

With Nicole and Joshua on holidays for the past ten days, he hadn't had a moment to call his own, certainly no time to drive out to the Double D and visit. In fact, just being here tonight was a tight fit.

Still, his brain reminded, Dani could have dropped in, phoned, written a note. But she hadn't. In fact, she'd all but disappeared, except for play practice.

And the sixty-four-thousand-dollar question was why. Second thoughts, cold feet, what? He had to know. So he waited for a chance to talk to her.

"It's good, isn't it? Very good." Miss Winifred plopped herself beside Dani, her eyes sparkling with anticipation.

"Yes, they've done a wonderful job. And the setting is marvelous, just as you said. I believe the evenings will be a real success." Dani gathered up her papers and stuffed them into her case without her usual regard for their precise organization.

In Luc's eyes that rush to leave was added proof that something was wrong. Instinct told him Dani wasn't fussed about some minor glitch in the play. It was something more personal that bothered her.

Him?

"I'm afraid I've got to run, Miss Win. I'm really swamped these days."

The words sounded forced even to Luc, fifty feet away.

"Are you, dear? I thought things might be a little quieter for you now." Winifred followed her across the room, her forehead creased in concern. "I understand you and Luc had a chat."

Dani stared at Miss Blessing, then shook her head. "Does nothing miss your eagle eyes?" she teased, but the sparkle was missing.

Luc took one step forward, then another. It was now or never.

"Nothing gets past those baby blues, does it, Miss Win?" He grinned at her, then turned to Dani, his heart-beat picking up its normal pace. "Well, Madame Director, how'd we do?"

"Great. Wonderful. The play is going to be a success." She didn't look at him.

"So should we set the time for the next practice?"

She blinked, then nodded, too obviously ill at ease with him nearby.

"Yes, of course. How silly of me." She raised her voice and announced a full dress rehearsal for the following week.

"Scene decorations and everything?" someone asked.

"Everything. If we've got problems with anything, I'd like to know about them sooner rather than later. Good night, everyone." She waved once, ducked her head and veered toward the door.

Miss Winifred's startled expression told Luc to follow.

"Dani?" He caught up with her at the side of the battered red truck. "Is something wrong?"

"Why would you ask that?" She yanked the door open and threw her case inside. "What on earth could possibly be wrong?"

Luc had enough emergency room experience to know the beginning signs of hysteria when he saw it. Dani's strained voice, the telltale blue streaks under her eyes, tense body and nervous hands told their own story. She was desperately worried about…something. He draped an arm around her shoulder.

"Come on. Let's go for a walk."

Dani held her ground. "I can't. I've got things to do at home."

"What things?" He had done something wrong, or else she was having second thoughts about kissing him.

"You wouldn't understand even if I took the time to explain. I just— I can't talk right now." She shrugged off his arm.

"Then, don't talk. We'll just walk and enjoy the park." He took her hand in his and tugged gently, urging her toward the lighted path that led to the lake. "You need a break, Dani. You're so tense you'll crack if you don't let go, even for just a few minutes. Don't think. Just walk. Doctor's orders."

She frowned, but obeyed.

The night was anything but silent. Crickets chirped, bullfrogs grumped. A few chickadees nattered at their babies. Voices, muted by the thick evergreens, hummed from the campgrounds beyond, while the last vestiges of a breeze kept tiny waves slapping onto the shore in a peace-inducing rhythm.

Luc walked along the crystal-white sand, vaguely surprised by the contentment that settled around his heart. Was this warm, gentle peace happening because Dani was here, beside him? Was that why it was enough just to let it flow through him, to hold her hand and know she was near?

It seemed they walked miles. Aeons later Luc became aware of her prolonged silence. What was wrong?

Half a mile down the beach, past giggling teenagers

and a couple lost in the wonder of each other's arms, Dani wrenched her hand out of his and sank to her knees on the fine white sand.

"Tired?" he asked, seating himself beside her, but careful to keep a minuscule distance between them. Maybe he was beginning to understand her, maybe it was because this was a private beach and he didn't want to cause gossip. Whatever excuse he used, Luc sensed that right now she needed time to consider her next words.

"Yes, I'm tired," she whispered.

The vehemence of the words surprised him.

"What's wrong, Dani?"

"Wrong?" She laughed, her voice oozing frustration. "I'm tired of trying to win something that can't be won. I'm tired of scheming and planning and working when it never seems to make a difference. Most of all, I'm so sick and tired of being tired. When will it be enough?" Her voice grew hoarse and she began coughing.

The rattle he heard emanating from her chest drew his attention. "Dani, are you sick?" He reached out to touch her forehead, but she reared away, her movements jerky, awkward.

Stung by her abrupt withdrawal, Luc let his hand drop to his side. Wasn't that proof enough that she wanted nothing more to do with him?

"I'm sorry." How did one apologize for caring? "I know your business is none of mine."

"No, it isn't. Apparently my business is Gray's." She laughed again, a harsh, broken sound, as her hands raked through her glossy dark curls. Her eyes were shiny with unshed tears as she stared out over the water.

He knew she held on to her control by only the slimmest of threads, knew also that she wouldn't thank him to notice. Luc turned his attention to her words.

"Gray's? What business? What are you talking about?"

Her lips twisted in a bitter smile. "The ranch. My problem. What else do I ever talk about with you?"

They'd talked about a lot of things, but now wasn't the time to mention it. Something big had happened and he wanted to know what it was.

"I thought you had the ranch situation almost under control."

Did that mean he wasn't the cause of her tears? Then, why was she avoiding him?

"So did I. It seems we were both wrong. Remember the diaries we brought back?"

It took him a minute to understand.

"Your father's diaries from the cabin. Yes, of course I remember them." How vividly he remembered that cabin. Just thinking about it resurrected the serenity he'd found there, as if he'd stepped into a glade of peace for one moment in time.

"I've been reading those diaries. All of them." She emitted a harsh laugh that held no mirth. "According to my father's own words, I owe Gray McGonigle for the land that cabin sits on. Dad borrowed the money from his father to buy it and never repaid the loan." Dani glared at him. "A thirty-two-year-old debt with interest. Do you have any idea how much that adds up to, even calculating a mere seven-percent interest?"

Luc shook his head, confused by what he'd just heard. Gray had never mentioned a loan.

"How much?" When she told him the amount she owed, he gulped.

"But how—"

"In his own words?" She tilted back her head, dashed away any trace of tears and stared into the night sky, reciting the words from memory. "'I gave Harris my precious Fancy Dancer as payment. Someday I'll buy it back, but for now the land is what counts. Dani's legacy.' My legacy." She turned her head to stare at him. "Isn't that rich? A legacy...of debt."

"And Fancy Dancer was a horse?"

Dani shrugged. "I'm assuming, though I don't understand how he thought one horse, even a prize one, would have been an even trade."

"You never saw this Fancy Dancer? Never heard of it before?"

She shook her head.

Luc frowned. "That's odd." How much should he tell her?

"Why odd?"

"Because before he died, your father talked about Fancy Dancer. At least, I think he did. I should probably check with Joshua before I say more, but I'm almost certain those were some of his last words. Dani and Fancy Dancer."

She stared at him, the hurt still glinting in the depths of her almond-shaped eyes. "Why tell me now? What use would a thoroughbred, if that's what Fancy Dancer was, be after all this time? Horses get old. Though I suppose..." Her voice died away as her mind grappled with the questions. After several moments of introspection, she sighed. "Not that it matters now. It doesn't. It happened and I'll have to deal with the consequences. But I can't help wondering if there was something... shady about this deal."

He shook his head. "I don't think your father would have been involved in something that wasn't honest,

Dani.'' Luc refused to believe it. ''He was always on the up-and-up. About everything.''

''Not always he wasn't,'' she muttered, her lips pursed. The betrayal showed in the softness of her words, in the slump of her narrow shoulders. ''He pretended my going to college wasn't a burden. Even when I asked outright how things were going, he never told me the truth.''

''He was protecting you.''

Her eyes blazed. ''He was lying to me.''

The anger finally poured out in a wave of tears, indignation that had been building up all through the hard months of saving the ranch. Luc's heart ached for her pain, but he didn't try to stop her. Far better to get this malaise out in the open. He knew from hard experience that once the bitterness was out, the healing could move in, cleanse and reclaim the memories.

''He lied about everything.'' Despair was etched deep in the whispered words.

Luc snapped to attention. ''Dani, that's not true.''

''Isn't it?'' She grimaced. ''I wish it weren't, but I've read everything in those diaries. Everything. My mother didn't die of some disease, Luc. She died of a broken heart—because my father wouldn't leave his precious land.''

''None of this makes sense. Your father loved your mother. What are you saying?'' He grabbed her arm and turned her to face him. ''Tell me.''

''Didn't he tell you? Well, guess what? Me neither.''

The bravado was a front. He glimpsed the fright and the wariness and knew her world had just been rocked off its foundations by something far deeper than a new debt.

She hiccuped a sob, but dredged up her courage and

poured out the rest of the story, though the pain of the words made her blanch.

"Dermot didn't tell you what?" He brushed the curls back from her forehead, searched her face. "Tell me, Dani. Please?"

"My mother was from New York. She'd never lived anywhere else. He met her there when he was working on the docks, raising money to buy a spread like his father's." Dani coughed again, then continued, her voice gravelly. "From the moment she set foot on that ranch, my mother hated it. The animals, the bugs, the heat, the cold. She couldn't seem to adapt."

"But he spoke about her as if—" Luc cut himself off, but too late.

"As if she was his true partner? Yes, I know. I listened to it for years. But according to my father's own words, she wasn't a rancher. She was an artist. The ranch isolated her. She continued her drawing and painting, but there was no one but him to see her work, no one to teach her new methods, no galleries to visit and no money to go back to New York. She was desperately homesick."

"But she had you! Surely that must have made a difference."

"At first I suppose it might have." Dani smiled sadly. "But I was a ranch girl, born and raised. I loved the horses, the cattle, the freedom. I started riding when I was two-and-a-half, and after that, my mother couldn't keep me inside. I sure wasn't interested in coloring in a book when there were cows to corral or colts to feed."

He didn't know what to say. This picture that she'd painted threw him for a loop. He'd always visualized Dani as a strong, self-sufficient woman who could take on whatever life handed her and still keep pushing forward. But now, now she seemed…defenseless, needy. The urge to shield her from any more hurt was strong, and Luc shifted an inch nearer, then realized what he was doing.

Trust, once lost, was hard to rebuild. She'd just had a lifetime of trust shaken bitterly, trust in the father she loved and revered. Why would she now trust Luc, a stranger, a transient? How could he expect her to lean on him, to draw on his strength, when he might not be here when she needed him again? He wanted her to see that he was not like her old boyfriend, or her father. But for Dani to depend on him, he'd have to be here. All the time.

Would that be so bad?

"Can you imagine how hard it must have been to cook meals for ranch hands and dust constantly, when all you wanted to do was paint and draw?" Dani leaned back on her hands, stared out across the water. "From the way he tells it, my mother simply lost her will to live. She gave up."

"I'm sorry." What else was there to say?

"So am I." Her eyes stared into a past he couldn't see. "You know, I can't even remember her. Not the way she smelled, or the touch of her hand, or her voice. Nothing. It's all blank. All I can remember is that stupid ranch."

She jumped to her feet and began walking back, her heels leaving deep indentations in the sand.

The beach was vacant now. The air had cooled, the voices had died away. They were all alone with only the wind whispering through the pines. Luc walked beside her, knowing he should reach out, yet afraid to in case she expected more than he could give. Finally they reached her truck.

"What will you do now?"

Dani shrugged. "I don't know. Legally the land is mine. The title's in my name."

"But morally—"

"I know. Morally I owe Gray. I wonder if he knows. Maybe I don't even need to tell him until I get things back on an even keel."

"I wouldn't dream of advising you one way or the other," he told her quietly. "This is your decision and you know the best way to deal with it. But I will say that Gray's in a tough place right now. Adam's back and making things difficult for Marissa and Gray."

"What's his complaint this time?"

"He's claiming Gray took part of his share of Harris's estate. If he had his own spread—"

"I am not giving that lazy lout my father's prime property!" Dani glared at him, anger lighting the gold flecks in her eyes. "Daddy loved that river property. It was very precious to him. Even if I had to turn over the rest, I'd keep that."

"I wasn't suggesting you hand it over. I was thinking more in terms of money. Gray knows Adam wouldn't work with him, but maybe if he had some extra cash coming in, Gray could put a down payment on a spread for his brother, give him some responsibility."

"As if Adam could handle that!" She sneered at the idea of it. "No. There's another way around this, I know it. I've just got to think this through before I go to Gray." She climbed into the truck, put her key in the ignition. Suddenly her hand froze. She glared at him. "I expect you to keep my confidence."

"Of course I will." But he didn't like the fix he was in. Gray was his friend. If the land rightly belonged to him, withholding information was wrong. And yet, how could he expect Dani to meekly hand over the one thing she had left, the thing she'd driven herself to keep?

Luc was stuck squarely in the middle between two very good friends. It wasn't a position he relished.

"I'd better get going." She coughed again, a rasping sound he'd heard before.

"You need something for that cold. Come and see me. Or Joshua, or Nicole if you want. Just don't let it get worse."

"It's just a silly summer cold, inconvenient and draining, but I'll be fine." She cranked the engine, revved it, but she didn't drive away.

Luc stood silent, waiting for whatever it was she clearly wanted to tell him.

"Luc, you may want to rethink the other night. I don't think I'm very good friend potential," she murmured at last. "I'm in hock up to my ears and not likely to get out soon. I can't promise anything."

"You don't have to." He leaned in through the open window and kissed her. "Someone gave me some good advice once." His fingers grazed the soft skin of her stubborn chin.

"Really?" Her hand smoothed the back of his hand. "Care to share?"

"They told me to visualize myself and where I wanted to be in five years. It's good advice." He kissed her again, then patted her cheek. His eyes widened as he realized she was running a temperature. "Dani, you're sick. Go home and get some sleep. God will take care of the rest—if you let Him."

One perfectly arched eyebrow tilted upward, but she only nodded.

"Where have I heard that before?" She shook her

head when he would have spoken. "Never mind. Good night, Luc. Good job tonight."

He grinned. "Terrific. If you don't count my notebook falling apart, stumbling across the stage, or the damage I did to Mrs. Mortimer's cake." He shook his head. "But I'll get it. I will get it. I'm determined not to blow this."

She smiled. "At least you're committed to the play."

He stared at her. Was that all he was willing to commit to? She sighed, and he realized he was keeping her from her bed.

"Good night, Dani. Take care."

"Yes." But her look seemed to ask, take care of what?

He stood back and watched as she drove away, then climbed into his own car.

"I'm trying, Lord, but You sure don't make it easy. I think I love that woman and now she's got a whole new set of problems. She's not going to have any time to think about me."

If she even wanted to, which Luc wasn't sure was a good idea anyway. Watching that play told him Dani was a woman with a future. The question was, did that future include him?

Chapter Nine

"How many times do we need to go through this before you figure out that building is not your thing?" Joshua tugged the nylon strand of surgical thread none too gently, pulling together the skin on Luc's injured forearm.

"Hey, take it easy!" Luc glared at him. "Your patients should have told you your bedside manner sucks, Joshua. Anyway, as if I haven't said it before—it was an accident."

"You said it was an accident last time, too," Joshua reminded, tying a knot in the final stitch. He snipped the thread, then took the roll of gauze Luc handed him and began winding it around the injured arm. "This particular accident cost you eight stitches, Doctor. Can't you just be content to learn your lines and wear your costume? Why is it necessary to touch an electric saw— about which you know less than nothing, I might add— and physically damage yourself?"

"I didn't intend—"

"Maybe not, but you sure scared the daylights out of

Big Ed. He almost broke my eardrum when he phoned. The sheriff told me he also broke every rule of safe driving on the books to get you here before you bled to death.''

"He exaggerates. So do you." Luc snipped the tape, pressed it into place, then reached out for his jacket. "I just nicked myself. It happens."

"Not to sensible people, it doesn't." Joshua sighed, shook his head as he put away his supplies. "Can't you think of some other way to impress her? Some men buy flowers. Perfume. Even dinner at a nice restaurant."

"Smart. Very smart." Luc winced as he slid his arm into the jacket, but masked his reaction quickly. He'd taken just about enough ribbing from Joshua about his construction abilities.

"Why don't you just admit you're in love with the woman and do something about it?"

Luc swung around, frustration building. "This advice is priceless, coming from a man who couldn't recognize love until she took off without him." He felt a tiny rub of satisfaction at the red wash over Joshua's cheeks. His friend had been goading him for days. Payback was overdue.

"Nicole *almost* took off," Joshua corrected gruffly. "I stopped her in time. And just because I was an idiot doesn't mean you have to copy. C'mon, man, you're a doctor. Smart, decisive. So make a decision. Do you love her? Then, get on with it. Might I suggest that your first order of business might be joining our partnership. Nicole's getting antsy."

"I am not." Nicole pushed through the office door and narrowed her eyes at them both. "I can hear everything you say, you know. Pregnancy doesn't make me deaf."

"Just a little tired and cranky," Joshua whispered in Luc's ear, then rose to kiss his wife on the cheek. "I was just telling Luc, we want his decision. Soon."

"He was nagging." Luc grinned at Nicole.

"How many stitches this time?" Nicole ignored his grin.

"Eight."

"Luc, this is ridiculous. Get in your car right now and drive out to the Double D. Ask her out for dinner or something."

"My advice exactly." Joshua crossed his arms over his chest, delighted with himself.

"Well, you can both forget your advice. I phoned on Monday to ask her out."

"And?" Two expectant faces waited.

"She didn't answer. I left a message. She didn't call back."

"So you try again."

"I did. Tuesday, Wednesday, and this morning. No response." He hated sounding like a little boy reciting his good deeds, but it was about time they put some of the blame on her. "Dani isn't interested."

"Interested in what?" Miss Winifred stood in the doorway. "Never mind. I know it's after hours, but I was hoping I'd catch you here. I need a favor, Lucas."

"What kind of a favor?" Suspicious of her timing, he studied her innocent expression. Miss Winifred had a habit of appearing at the oddest moments. Tonight she had that glint in her eyes. "Didn't I tell you to cut down on the late nights? You'll wear yourself out."

"I can sleep anytime. Besides, this is important."

"What is?" Nicole moved to stand beside her. "How can we help?"

"Every Thursday Dani comes to town. It's her ritual.

She does all her errands, buys a few dozen doughnuts, then takes them over to the senior center for a visit.'' She paused. ''She didn't come today.''

''So?'' Luc shrugged, but in a corner of his mind he remembered that rasping cough. ''She's probably busy.''

''Gray hasn't seen her either, not for the past three days. She wasn't at church on Sunday. In fact, the last place anyone saw her was at practice last week. Saturday night.'' She waited, a certain expectation on her face as her focus remained on Luc.

He checked his watch. ''It's way after nine o'clock, Miss Win. I can't show up at her door at this time of night.''

She said nothing, merely waited, her face implacable. Luc knew that look. She wasn't about to let him off the hook. Not that he wanted to be let off. He'd had a niggling voice in the back of his mind all day today that insisted he'd feel better if he knew for himself that Dani was all right.

''Fine. I'll go. At least I'm not on call.'' He ignored the glances full of innuendo passing among the other three and grabbed his bag. ''If she reams me out, I'm blaming you. All of you.''

They said nothing.

Luc stopped by his office, snatched up several cold-medication samples a rep from a pharmaceutical company had left, and tossed them in his bag, all the while conscious of the whispers behind him. Let them whisper. He had things to do.

If ever a night was perfect, this one was. The wind had died earlier so that now the heat of the day had waned to a softness that feathered over the skin in delightful coolness. As his car purred over the highway that led to her road, he saw the moon, fat and orange, just cresting the horizon. The night was bright, the way clear.

Someone with a grader had recently been down the road leading to the Double D. Luc was able to press the accelerator down without the bone-jarring thuds he'd experienced before. Twice he had to slam on the brakes, once for a deer that dashed across the road, once for a portly skunk and her babies. Nobody in their right mind rushed a skunk.

Once past the obstacles, he resumed his speed, anxious now to get to the ranch. Apprehension chewed at him. There was something wrong. He could feel it.

The yellow glow from a light high up a pole was strangely comforting to Luc as he pulled into the yard. Until he noticed the battered red truck parked haphazardly on the bit of lawn she usually kept mowed. The house was completely dark.

"I'll wake her up and she'll tear a strip off me for sticking my nose in," he grumbled, taking the steps two at a time. "She'll probably read me the riot act." He rapped on the door, hard. "Dani?"

No answer.

"Dani, it's me, Luc. Are you okay?" No light switched on, no sound of footsteps assured him that she was on the way. A noise from the corral behind him drew his attention. He squinted.

Duke pranced around the fence, pawing once or twice. Then he whinnied, but it wasn't his usual greeting.

Why was the horse out? Dani always kept him inside the stable at night. He hit the door again, harder, more insistent as the little kernel of worry grew.

"Dani? Answer the door?"

A sound, something too soft to clearly identify, came from within the house. That made up his mind. He twisted the handle, and when it opened, he let himself inside.

"Dani, it's Luc. Where are you?"

A sound, garbled and low, came from the study. He followed it.

"Dani?" He stopped. Stared.

She lay on the couch swaddled in blankets, her face pasty, eyes glassed over. He strode across, laid a hand on her forehead, then pursed his lips.

"Why didn't you call me, Dani?"

She blinked, tried to focus as she raised herself on one elbow. "Luc? Hi. Don't feel too well. Practice without me." The words were barely audible. She spoke in a gruff whisper, then slumped back into her nest of blankets. "Cold."

Thankful for the rigid training that made him take his bag everywhere, he snapped it open and pulled out a thermometer. One hundred and four degrees. Her skin was hot and dry, her lips blistered. An empty glass and tipped-over pitcher lay on the floor beside the sofa. He nudged her mouth open, stared down her throat. His eyes took it all in as his hands reached for his stethoscope.

"I'm just going to listen to your lungs," he murmured, unbuttoning the top button of her shirt. "Breathe in, Dani."

He didn't need more than one breath to tell him what he'd already guessed. Pneumonia.

"Come on, Dani. We need to get you to Blessing and into the hospital." He tried to scoop her tiny body into his arms, but she jerked away, then flopped down, wheezing.

"Can't go," she told him. She shook her head for added emphasis.

"You have to. You've got pneumonia and you've let it progress. I can treat you in the hospital."

She shook her head, her eyes closed. "No." She swallowed, then spoke. "No insurance."

"That doesn't matter. They'll work something out." He tried to lift her again but she wouldn't let him.

"No charity," she rasped, then a coughing fit took away all her breath and she could only lie there, gasping.

"Oh, man," he muttered. But he knew taking her there against her will wouldn't help. He'd have to treat her here.

Moving quickly, he found a vein and set up a drip, glad he'd kept a spare in his bag after learning that practicing medicine in Blessing meant being prepared for anything. The saline solution was an extra, left over from treating a patient forty miles away who'd cut his foot at a sawmill.

Dani watched him with glazed eyes, but without protest. Once the solution was dripping steadily, he filled a syringe, then emptied the antibiotics into her bloodstream, mentally going through the protocols as he worked. Next the fever.

"Thirsty," Dani said. "Please."

"Okay. Stay here. Don't move." When he was certain she understood, Luc went to the kitchen. Her throat was raw. He ruled out the orange juice and lemonade, shut the fridge. Tea. Peppermint tea, he decided. She drank it all the time. He'd make it lukewarm and grind the pills into it.

It took several minutes to prepare the drink. All during that time, he kept his attention on the next room, listening for sounds of distress. Dani seemed asleep.

When he returned he roused her gently, held the cup to her lips. She twisted her head away, but he held it steady. "Drink, Dani. It's tea. It'll help."

She sipped, made a face. "Funny tea," she said huskily.

His heart ached for the pain she was in. Why was that? He'd treated thousands of patients, and had always been able to maintain a professional detachment. But with this tiny, fragile woman, he sensed every ache.

"Drink some more, honey," he whispered, propping her shoulders against his arm as he held the cup to her lips. "Sip, come on. That's the way. A little more now."

When she turned her head away, refusing more tea, he let her go. Almost immediately she began coughing, fighting to draw breath into her lungs.

"Sit up, Dani. That's better. Just relax and let the cough move through you. Okay." He waited until the spasm passed, then let her lie back as his cell phone rang.

"Luc? What's going on?"

"She's got pneumonia, Nicole. Her lungs don't sound good."

"So you're bringing her in?"

"She won't go." He turned away, hoping Dani couldn't hear. "She doesn't have any insurance and she refuses to go to the hospital for what she calls charity. Arguing just made her weaker, so I've set up an IV and shot her full of Erythromycin. Right now I'm trying to get her fever down."

"Do you want help?"

"Not now. I wish I had some oxygen, but I'll manage.'' He turned, checked her color. Was it better? ''I can stay tonight. That's no problem. Besides, it's too late to call anyone else. But if you could find someone who'd nurse her tomorrow, I could catch a break. Anyway, I think it would be better, given the local gossips.''

''I'll take care of it. Phone me after seven to tell me if you need anything else. I'll send it along.''

''Okay. Thanks, Nici.'' He picked up Dani's hand, checked her pulse. ''Are you there?''

''Yes, I'm here. Just thinking.''

''About what?''

''That's the first time you've called me Nici since you came. It sounds good. It's the kind of thing partners and friends do. Which is what we want, Luc. You do know we want you to join us, don't you?''

''Yeah, I know.''

''Good.'' Silence. Then she spoke again, this time in a quiet, serious tone. ''This might be a good time for you and Dani to talk, Luc. Or at least, you can talk. She'll have to listen. She can't go anywhere.''

''Thanks, Nici.'' He snapped the phone closed, grinned, then rearranged Dani's blankets, checked her temperature, coaxed a few more drops of treated tea down her throat. When he'd done everything he could to make her more comfortable, Luc prepared himself for the long night ahead.

''Daddy? Where are you?''

Dani fought to free herself of the suffocating blanket of darkness that wouldn't let her breathe. A hand, cool, gentle, helped her sit up. She coughed over and over, gasping for breath.

''It's okay. Take it easy. You're fine.''

''Luc?'' She squinted up into the light.

"Uh-huh." He was doing something to her arm.

Dani glanced down, surprised to see the needle.

"What's that?"

"Just something to make you feel better. Is it working? I took the IV out yesterday." He stood and stared down at her for so long that she shifted finally, uncomfortable.

"I—I guess." She swallowed, realized it didn't hurt nearly as much as it had. "What time is it?"

He grinned. "What difference does it make?"

"The horses." Dani forced herself upright, though she would far rather have cuddled into her blankets and gone back to sleep. "I have to look after the horses."

"Gray's already done that. In fact, your friends have taken care of all your chores."

"But I didn't want—"

"I know. You wanted to do it yourself. Well, this time you couldn't. You've been very sick, Dani. And until you're completely better, I don't want you moving out of this room."

His scowl bothered her. What did Luc know about ranching?

"There's hay to get in. Otherwise I won't have any feed next year." She finally worked her legs free, stared down at her pajamas in dismay. "Who—?"

"Miss Winifred. She's been caring for you for the past three days, on and off."

"Three days!" She couldn't believe it. How could three days go by without her noticing?

"I came out Thursday night. I should have taken you to the hospital, but you refused."

"No insurance. I'm better off here anyway." She nodded, her neck weary of supporting her head. Why was she so weak?

"Dani, you could have died! Or at the least, made yourself sicker than you needed to be. I told you last week to come into the office."

He was doing it again, glaring at her as if she'd done something to offend him. Dani ignored Luc, for the moment, and concentrated on making the room stop spinning.

"It was just a cold." Dani refocused. That was better.

"No, it wasn't just a cold. It was much more serious. You have pneumonia." He hunkered down beside the sofa, drew her chin down so she had to look at him. "This has got to stop."

"What?"

"This business of alienating yourself from people who care about you."

"I'm not doing that." She wrenched her chin away from him, tears of helplessness rolling down her cheeks. "I just needed to deal with this latest setback in my own way."

Luc was shaking his head.

"What? You don't believe me?"

"Nope. I think it goes way deeper than that."

"Really? And now I suppose you're going to psychoanalyze me."

He looked pained by her words, and she was immediately sorry that she'd said them, but she'd had to say something to keep the fear at bay. Now the ugliness hung between her and the doctor like icicles.

"I'm not a psychiatrist, Dani. But I do care about you and I can't stand by and watch you do this any longer."

"Exactly what is it you think I'm doing?"

"Building walls. The Double D is like your own little island, and you've isolated yourself here, in the center, protected, where you think no one can hurt or betray you again.'' His hand slipped over hers. ''It's like you've filled a little moat around yourself to keep everyone away.''

''My, aren't you picturesque.'' Scorn laced her voice but it couldn't hide the truth. His words ate like acid through the shroud of protection she'd tried to build for herself.

She knew exactly what he meant. Distrust colored every encounter with people lately. Wariness that something else waited to bowl her over with cares and worries had made her withdrawn. And now even Luc had become a threat. Why?

What had he ever done but be her friend?

He'd made her see herself from a new perspective. Not as an independent woman meeting life on her own terms, but as a scared rabbit, running from everyone and everything that threatened.

''Dani? I'm sorry if I've hurt you.'' That perpetual lock of disobedient hair flopped over one brown eye. ''I wasn't trying to. That's the last thing I want. It's just— You've got to trust someone, Dani. You can't go through life alone. Nobody can.'' In his sincerity, Luc reached out, squeezed her fingers.

She relished the contact for thirty seconds, then drew her hand away. It didn't seem to bother him.

''You have to start building bridges, meeting people halfway, trust that they won't hurt you, and that even if they do, God will give you the strength to get up and try again.''

Luc was building a bridge. He'd reached out to her over and over, offered his help, his shoulder to lean on, his ear to listen. He'd made it clear that he cared about her, wanted to develop their relationship. But she was the one who kept pulling back.

Even now, the thought of exposing her whole soul to him, letting him see how deeply her father's betrayal went, filled her with trepidation. She was the strong one. Dani could always be counted on.

When she didn't speak, Luc sighed heavily, then rose to his feet.

"Your temperature is down, your lungs are almost clear. I think you should be able to get up and around in a couple of days."

"Thank you."

"That doesn't mean you can go back to doing the work of three people. You can't. For the sake of your health, you're going to have to accept your neighbors' help."

She opened her mouth to thank him, but he misunderstood and held up one hand.

"There is no discussion. That's the way it's going to be."

"Fine."

It took him a minute to absorb her answer, but finally he nodded. His eyes moved around the room.

"Dani, what happened to all the furniture in this house?"

She flushed, kept her head bowed. "There's plenty of furniture."

He stood in front of her, waiting until she looked at him.

"The big credenza thing that was in the hall is gone. So are the buffet and hutch from the dining room and a whole lot of other things. Those things were antiques. I hope you didn't—" He stopped, frowned. "You sold them, didn't you."

"They were mine to do with as I please, Luc," she reminded curtly. "Yes, I sold them. What good are they sitting here when I could lose the ranch? I got an appraisal which I thought was fair, so I sold them."

"To pay Gray." He shook his head. "Oh, Dani, I wish I knew what to do about you." He sank down beside her and pulled her into the circle of his arms. "I'm sorry I ragged on you. It must have hurt to watch them go."

Holding her close, he let out a deep breath.

At first surprised by his embrace and a little wary, after a moment Dani allowed herself to relax and enjoy the feeling of being protected, cared for. It had been so long.

It's so easy for him, Lord. He just naturally gives. Help me to give back. Help me to trust. Take away the barriers. Don't let me hurt him. But most of all, God, protect me. Don't let him hurt me.

"It's okay, Luc," she whispered after a long time. "They were just things. I'd rather have the ranch without them than lose the ranch with them."

"I guess. But they were special things that you treasured." He pushed the lank, listless hair away from her face. "You scared me, Danielle DeWitt. You scared the very life out of me." His palm lay against her forehead for a moment, then slid down to cup her cheek. "Why are you so proud and stubborn? Why won't you let anybody inside?"

"There's nothing much to see," she replied, unsure of what to say and afraid to ruin the moment.

Luc held her away from him so that he could see her face. "That's nonsense. You're a woman of character, Dani. You don't give up, or back off, or take the easy way out. You give and give. Why can't you, just once, take something?''

''Like what?''

His mouth opened as if to speak, but then he seemed to think better of it. Instead, Luc leaned forward.

''Like me,'' he whispered, and then he kissed her.

''Luc?'' She lifted her hand, ran her finger down the side of his neck.

He clamped his hand over hers. ''Dani?'' He stared into her eyes. ''You told me to look into the future. Shall I tell you what I see?'' He gave a low chuckle. ''My vision is getting a little clearer each day. Want to know why?''

Hesitantly, she nodded.

''When I look into the future, I see you, Dani. I wake up with ideas I never had before, I feel emotions I never expected, dreams I didn't know existed inside my head.''

''You're scaring me.''

''You think you're scared?'' He refused to let her pull away but drew her closer. ''I haven't slept in three days. I've been thinking of the future, my future, and then I'd look down and imagine you not there. I was terrified.''

She pulled back. ''Don't stay in Blessing because of me, Luc.'' She shook her head when he tried to bring her against him again. ''It wouldn't be right…you have your own goals…I'll have to move, leave…''

She couldn't help herself, she swooned into his kiss. Pliant and warm, his lips covered hers. Her arms slipped around him as she drifted on the magic of the moment. She was safe here, secure.

She didn't want to leave.

A tear squeezed from the corner of her eye, trickled

down her cheek. He followed the trail back from temple to eyelid, then moved to her lips.

"I didn't mean to hurt you, Dani."

Oh, God, I've let him get too close. I can't love him. Not now. Not when there's no future in it.

"I have to tell you something, Luc."

He nuzzled her neck, his breath warm against her skin. "Can't it wait? I'd like to continue where we left off."

So would she, but instead she eased back.

"We can't. I can't." She took a deep breath. "I'm leaving town, Luc. As soon as the play's over, I intend to leave Blessing."

Chapter Ten

Luc couldn't believe he'd heard right.

"Leaving? Why?" He studied her, his heart awhirl with confusion.

"There's no future for me here."

The words struck his heart. He could almost hear it crack. All the waiting, wondering, biding his time—and the truth was, she didn't love him. Not enough to stick around.

"When the check comes from the furniture dealer, I'll have just about enough to pay Gray the original price of the land."

"So you stay, raise some more."

"How?" She shook her head, touched his lips with her fingertip. "There's nothing more to sell, nothing more I can do. I'm not a rancher, Luc. I never was. I only tried to hang onto the Double D because my father wanted me to have it."

"What's changed? Nothing. It's still your ranch."

"Everything's changed." She told him the plans she'd made in the hours before the virus attacked.

"When I get my strength back, I'm going to have to talk to Gray, explain everything. I won't blame him if he's angry, if he wants the land back."

"He won't—"

"Let me finish. Please?" She waited until he nodded, then continued.

"You're a doctor. You belong in Blessing. People love you and you love them."

"They love you, too."

She shook her head. "It's not home anymore, Luc. Not my home. I was away too long, I guess."

"So you do something else." He wasn't letting her go. Not like this. There had to be a way. There had to be.

"What can I do, Luc? I never finished college. But even if I had, there's no place in Blessing that would buy my stories."

"Dani, you belong in Blessing." *With me.*

She shook her head, her smile sad. "I thought I did. I thought it was the one place on earth that was truly home. But I was wrong. Life goes on, plans adapt to fit the circumstances."

"But—"

She sealed his lips with hers, then tipped backward against his arm, her finger tracing the features on his face as if she thought she could memorize them.

"You belong in Blessing, Lucas Lawrence. This is your home, these are your people. You fit." Dani threaded her fingers through his hair, laughed sadly. "Look at you, rumpled and half-dead on your feet, but here you are fussing about me. You were born to be a doctor, and God led you here to fulfill His purpose. I just haven't found mine yet."

"Maybe your purpose is to help me," he stated

boldly. What was the point in pretending anymore? He was crazy about this woman.

She laughed at him.

"I'm no nurse, Luc. I can't stand the sight of blood and needles make me nauseated. Besides that, I owe more money than you could imagine. What good would I be to you?" Dani hugged him tightly for one short minute, then eased away so that Luc was forced to his feet.

"What could I say to make you stay?"

"Oh, Luc." She rose, a bit shaky as she found her balance.

Luc slipped an arm around her, drew her close. Her own arms circled his waist as if they belonged there. She rested her head on his chest.

"Please don't ask me to stay here. Don't make this any harder."

"It's already hard." He heard the tears in her voice, and told himself to back off. But he couldn't. This was his future.

"It can't work for us, Luc. I wish it could. But you've got your own debts from medical school. When you sign on with the Darlings, you'll be taking on even more. You've already done so much to be part of this community, I won't add my problems. I can't."

"I'd gladly share any of your problems. All of them. You know that."

She shook her head. "No. It wouldn't work."

He didn't understand it. Why would God have given him this love, allowed it to blossom and bloom, when there was no future in it? Was he supposed to learn something? What?

"It doesn't make sense, Dani. You can't run away now, not now." He was determined to make her see his heart. "How can you expect me to just let go, give up my hopes, my dreams? I don't understand how you can ask that—not if you care about me."

"Oh, Luc, I care. I care so much! But I can't, don't you see?"

"No." He clung to her, trembling at the sensations that rolled through him when he thought of never holding her again. Never be near her, wrap her in his arms, touch her silken cheek, feel her hair tickle his chin. How could he stand back and let her walk away, pretend his heart didn't ache for her?

He kissed her as he'd only allowed himself to dream of kissing her. And wonder of wonders, she kissed him back, withholding nothing, sharing her feelings so openly that he couldn't pretend not to understand that she cared about him.

"Stay. Please stay. With me," he whispered, when at last he could breathe again. "I know it looks hopeless. We haven't had time to figure out how to make it work. I'm just asking you to give us that chance."

Dani eased out of his arms, her face sad. She walked across the room, peered out the window at the dull gray sky. Finally she turned around, decision written across her face.

"I'll stay until after the play, Luc. But that's the best I can do. I've done a lot of thinking about this."

Hope bubbled inside. *A lot of thinking?* She'd known she cared about him for a while? He could have kicked himself for wasting time.

"So have I," he admitted.

"Then, you must realize that hoping for something between us is impossible."

"I don't see that at all. Besides, there's already something between us," he reminded her.

She blushed, stared at the floor. "Yes, well, there can't be anything else. We're too far apart. You've got—how many years of medical school?" She didn't wait for his answer, but shook her head. "I never even finished college. You've traveled all over this country. I've hardly been anywhere."

Luc was about to interrupt, but her words forced him to stop, reconsider. He'd been right to worry. The age thing bothered her, too.

"There's got to be a world out there where I can fit in." Her voice sounded a little too cheerful. "God must have a place for me. It's not here, I know that. Maybe once I've moved on—"

"Stop it, Dani." He grabbed his bag, slapped his stethoscope and other paraphernalia inside, trying to stem his fury. "I don't want to hear about it. This isn't like you. You see the first sign of trouble and run? Well, I can't stop you. The truth is, I don't think I want to. If you stayed you'd only blame me for your unhappiness."

It was all a heap of nonsense. But Luc had run out of ideas to make her see what was so evident to him.

She was *the one*.

He knew it as clearly as he knew his own name. Dani DeWitt was the only woman he'd ever met who could make him blazingly furious while, at the same time, he wanted to kiss her. He wanted her in every possible way there was for a man to want a woman—as a friend, a partner, by his side, in his heart, a permanent fixture in his life. A wife.

But him wanting that wasn't enough. She had to want it too. And she didn't.

Not enough to try and find a way through the problems. Not enough to stick around and work out a compromise.

"What are you doing?"

"Packing up my stuff. I've got to see some other patients." More lies.

"I'm sorry, Luc. I didn't mean to hurt you."

That stung. He dropped his bag on the floor, whirled around and advanced on her until she'd backed up against the sofa and his nose was inches from hers.

"I think you do mean to hurt. Because it's the easy way out." He swallowed hard, then took the plunge. "I'm not taking the easy way out anymore, Dani. You say God sent me here and I believe you. Tonight I'm going to start talking to Nicole and Joshua about that partnership."

"Good."

"Yes, it is good. I've wandered around, waited for some heavenly sign and wasted a couple of years trying to find exactly what I have right here in Blessing. This is home. I belong here." He took a deep breath. "I also belong with you. I love you the same way a thousand other men have loved a certain woman all through the ages. You're like my other half. You make me a better person, a better doctor, a better man. I need you to be there when I can't tell anyone else what's eating me. I need to hold and care for you. I need you to know that I'm not going anywhere, that I won't let you down, that you can always depend on me."

"Luc—"

"I'm staying, Dani. I want to make a home, get married, have a family, do all the normal things every other guy my age wants to do. And I want to do it with you. Can you believe that? I'm thirty-four and you're the first woman I've ever proposed to."

He checked her response. Dani's jaw had dropped. Her eyes were wide.

"P-proposed?" she squeaked.

"As in marriage." He'd expected a reaction, a protest, something. But Dani simply stood there, staring at him as if he'd lost his mind. Well, maybe he had. But the time had come to deal in truth. "Well?"

"I— I can't, Luc." Tears welled in her eyes, but her shaking head told him her answer. "I have to go. After the play. I'm sorry."

"So am I. We could have made something wonderful, Dani. We could have shared something a lot of people don't get a chance at. But to do that, you'd have to stick around. You'd have to trust me not to mess up, and when I do, you'd have to be able to forgive me." He turned, walked back to pick up his bag, then moved toward the door. Once there, he stopped, turned back.

"Miss Winifred will be out to check on you this afternoon. She's been a real help. I'd appreciate it if you didn't keep her too long. She's a bit tired these days."

Dani nodded.

"You have to let go of the fear, Dani. It's keeping you from the joy."

Luc turned on his heel and walked out of the farmhouse. The ride home seemed short to him. There was a lot to muse on. Suddenly everything seemed to have fallen into place.

Dani DeWitt might have turned him down cold, but he wasn't about to let her get away without a fight. He simply had to decide on the right course of action.

Okay, Lord. You want me here, I'm here. And I'm staying until You tell me to go. But what can I do about Dani?

The answer was a long time coming.

Chapter Eleven

A week later, Dani laid the bills out on the table in front of her, lining the hundreds, fifties and twenties in precisely organized rows. The check from her mother's wedding gift, a full set of Limoges china, had arrived today and she'd cashed it earlier, scurrying in and out of town like a frightened rabbit, afraid she'd meet Luc.

Now she counted each pile, a smile of pure relief tugging at her heart as she came to the last stack. There was enough to pay Gray the amount she'd *guesstimated* as the cost of the land, plus a few dollars left over to start out her new life. She'd kept her father's trust, gone far beyond her original plan to fulfill his belief in her.

So maybe she wouldn't be able to work his land, run his horses, build on his work. But she hadn't lost the land. Not yet, anyway.

Not unless Gray refused her proposal.

Her knees wobbled at the prospect of asking.

She'd never asked for a favor like this one, never felt as if her life hung in the balance while someone else debated over her future. Doing it now scared her. Wild scenarios sprang to mind. But Luc had left her with one thing, and that was her certainty that she had to depend on God. Only He could work things out now. Only He could coax Gray's heart into accepting her suggestion.

So what was she waiting for? Why didn't she go to Gray, tell him the truth and wait for God to work?

Dani avoided the questions by rolling the money together and stuffing it inside an old cookie jar that sat atop the cabinets in the kitchen. It looked like an ornament. No thief would think to look there.

She'd barely returned the ladder to its peg in the basement when someone rapped on the back door. Dani hurried upstairs, heart in her throat as she pulled open the door. She could only stare.

Brad Conway stood on the doorstep, his handsome mouth tipped up in a grin. "Hey, babe."

Dani just stared. He had the grace to look embarrassed. But that was all. No apology, no regrets for what he'd done to her. Just that brash, devil-may-care shrug that told her he'd put the past behind them. Her blood pressure surged.

"Where've you been, Dani? Professor Dean said you didn't come back after Christmas. You weren't there for convocation, either."

"I didn't graduate, Brad." She had to push the words out. "I couldn't. Remember?"

He cocked his head. "Dani, you wrote six plays a week in those days. You could have done another one. But to drop out with only a few classes to go—" He shook his head. "What were you thinking?"

There were so many answers to that arrogant question. But Dani didn't have the stomach or the energy to address any of them. What was the point? It was over, done with. She was ready to move on, start over. Why did he have to show up now?

She let her eyes move over him, saw the familiar easy grace of his stance against her door, the charming smile, the twinkle of his blue eyes. She waited for the shaft of pain, the brittle hurt that always came when she remembered his betrayal.

It was a different kind of pain.

Dani blinked, refocused. The indignation, the fury, the hurt pride—all of that still boiled up inside. But in the deepest part of her, her heart didn't flinch. In the course of true love, Brad and his sad little game of treachery simply didn't matter anymore. Why was that?

Luc's face swam into her mind, his chocolate-brown eyes melting as he told her he cared about her. Luc was everything Brad could never be. Because of Luc and the lessons he'd taught her, Brad had lost some of his power to hurt her. For that alone she would always be grateful to Luc.

"What do you want, Brad?"

He shrugged. "A chat. A visit. Like the old days." He glanced over his shoulder, scanning the hills and valleys now bursting in their verdant prime. "This is quite the place."

"It's my place. And I've got work to do. If you want to chat with someone, why don't you look up some of your old cronies? You and they have so much in common."

"That's cold, Dani. Even for you." He waited, obviously expecting her to apologize. "You always did think you were one step above us, didn't you."

"At least I didn't steal your work." Dani caught sight of Luc's car carefully negotiating the lane. Despite everything that had happened between them, she was delighted to see him. Especially now.

"That's a friend of mine. We've got some plans." She hadn't even known Luc was coming, but now that he was here, she didn't intend to let him leave until Brad was safely off the ranch. He might have fooled her once, but he wouldn't do it a second time. He sure wasn't going to learn anything about this play.

"A boyfriend?" Brad's eyebrows rose as he watched the car pull up next to the house. He stared even more when Luc climbed out of his car.

"Hi, Luc." Dani could hardly miss the way the doctor's eyes flared when they landed on her. Then he glanced at Brad.

"Am I interrupting?"

"Of course not. We'll go for our ride, just as I promised." She hadn't promised anything, and Luc knew it, but he also knew when to remain silent. "This is Brad, Brad Conway. You may remember I told you about him."

"Oh, I remember." Luc's eyes narrowed to black pinpoints as they rested on the other man.

"Brad, this is Dr. Lucas Lawrence. He's a friend of mine."

"Doctor?" The arrogant eyebrow moved a fraction higher, then slid back to stare at Dani. "Have you been sick?"

"Yes, but that's not why Luc is here. We go riding together. We have an appointment today." Could she make the hint to leave more obvious?

"Actually, that's why I'm here. I've got to cancel. I was just over at Gray's. Adam injured himself. I've got to get back to town and do some stitching. They've taken him to the hospital." He wished he could make her understand what his heart knew. But words had never been his strong suit. "How are you?"

"Fine. Perfectly fine. Making plans for the future." She wouldn't let him get his hopes up. What was the point? "I'll see you later, then?" she murmured, meaning the play practice, but refusing to say it. With the way things were going, Brad would take it into his head to show up.

"Of course. We've only got a few days left before the big day. We need you back in charge."

She nodded. "I'll be there."

"It's going to be a success, Dani. A raging success that the county will be in a furor about for years to come. Those kids will get their orphanage, and it's all due to you."

"Not all." She tore her gaze from his, checked over one shoulder. Brad was listening avidly. "We can talk later," she said, inclining her head just a little to show Luc that she didn't want to give anything away.

Luc frowned, stared at her for several moments, then turned to look at Brad. She saw the exact moment he realized that she didn't want her college friend to know about the play. Then he looked back at her and shook his head. Determination washed across his features, his chin lifted.

"Brad, you might be interested in seeing some of Dani's work staged. Why don't you come to our practice tonight? Ask anyone in town. They'll give you directions. We start at eight."

Brad's blue eyes sparked to life. "Hey, I'd like that. I'm staying at the local motel. They'll know the way, won't they?" He glanced at Dani, but finding no answers there, looked at Luc.

"They'll know."

"Great. I'll see you later, then." He loped across the porch, jumped off and hurried to his sports car. Not two minutes later he was tearing down the dusty road, leaving only a thin red trail of dust behind.

"Why did you do that?" Dani demanded. "He stole my last play, or have you forgotten that?"

Luc's lips lifted in a tender smile that made her skin prickle with awareness.

"I haven't forgotten, Dani. But you can't hide from him."

"But I don't have to make it easy for him, either," she muttered, disgusted. "What's that verse about casting pearls before swine?"

"What are you getting so worked up about? Are you afraid he'll steal this one, too?"

"He could." She glared at him. "He has no scruples, you know."

Luc shook his head. "Oh, Dani, the problems you create by living in fear." One hand reached out, touched her cheek, brushed the hair away. "You wouldn't tell anyone that you wrote that play, and now that decision's coming back to haunt you. If Brad does get his hands on a copy, who's to know he didn't write it?"

He was dead on and he knew it. Dani bit her bottom lip to keep from ranting at him. If he knew all that, why had he told Brad to come? Didn't he care?

One look into his eyes gave her all the answer she needed.

"People will do what they'll do, sweetheart. You can't stop them. You can only go on living your life. Why not let him see that you aren't cowed by his betrayal, that you can still produce work but he can only steal? Why not trust that God can take care of all of this?"

"How will God take care of somebody like Brad?"

"I don't know. He wouldn't be God if He had to explain to you and me. But the hiding away, the keeping secrets, walking around on tiptoes—" he shook his head "—I can't be part of that, Dani. I won't let you do it, either. Not as long as I can stop it. You've created a wonderful, funny, heart-wrenching story that needs to be shared. Why let someone like Brad What's-his-name ruin that? Why run and hide?"

She didn't know how it happened, but a moment later she was in his arms and he was kissing her. Dani responded because there was nothing else she could do. Whenever he kissed her, her brains left and her emotions took over.

When Luc finally released her enough to catch her breath, she knew it had been a mistake to let him get so close. Temptation to change her mind, to stay in Blessing, on the ranch, almost swayed her—until she remembered how easily Brad had conned her less than a year ago.

"I've made my plans, Luc. I won't change them. I'm still leaving Blessing."

"I know." Using his forefinger, he traced a path over her eyebrows, down her nose, over her lips, to her chin. "You're proud and beautiful and you have so much to give. Can't you reach out a little, build a tiny bridge of trust? Just take the first step, Dani. I won't let you down."

Everyone let someone down at one time or another. Even Luc. And that would break her heart.

She shifted, moved away, kept her eyes on the ground. "I'm sorry. I wish it could be different."

"I'm not giving up, Dani. I'm praying hard."

"For what?" she whispered.

"A way for God to get past your doubts." He glanced at his watch. "I've got to go."

"Luc?"

"Yes?" He faced her, a question on his face.

"I, um, need to talk to Gray."

"You haven't told him about the diary yet?" He frowned, seeing the answer on her face. "You should have done that as soon as you knew, Dani."

"Why? I didn't have an answer then. Now I do. Which is why I need to see him. Soon."

He waited, eyes alert.

"The furniture and my mother's china brought in enough to pay for the original purchase price. I'm going to offer Adam the Double D to rent. I'll get a job to pay off the interest. If Gray will agree." She felt a tiny squiggle of warmth that she'd been able to handle the entire matter without anyone's help.

"And if he won't?"

She shrugged, unable to tell him that she refused to consider that. "I'll think of something else."

As he stood there gazing at her, a faint smile played over his mouth. " 'The best laid plans...gang aft agley,' " he murmured.

"What?"

"I mean, I don't think it will be that easy, Dani. I think God's going to give you second thoughts on this one."

"Oh." He knew something. She could see it in the way his shoulders sloped as he leaned against the open door. He seemed almost...happy? "What aren't you saying, Luc?"

"Adam McGonigle was practicing his calf-roping skills. He got thrown into a barbed-wire fence. He won't be running anything for a while. Not with that back."

Luc bent, brushed his mouth over hers, then headed toward his car.

Dani let the door swing shut. She needed to rethink. Adam's injury created problems. But then, she already had those. Especially with Brad on the scene.

So now what?

Chapter Twelve

That night Luc watched from stage left as the bustle of set decorators arranged their work in its proper order on the pulley system Big Ed had concocted to facilitate change of scenes. The man was truly a genius when it came to anything like this, though it had taken him a good chunk of time to get the operation as smooth as he wanted.

"How's it look?" Gray stood behind him, watching.

"If it works, it'll be great. If it doesn't..." He let it hang, knowing that the entire production was in God's hands. The Father knew what they were trying to do. He knew the problems they'd had. Luc only wished Dani could accept that and let Him handle it.

"It'll work." Gray moved a cord out of the way, shifted some props, then nodded. "Everything up here seems shipshape." He glanced over Luc's shoulder, then paused. "You know that guy?"

"What guy?" Luc held his breath as the cable squeaked and the backdrop for the church scene shivered ominously.

"The one trying to hide in the back."

Luc glanced over. Nodded. "Dani knows him. Some guy from her college days. He stopped by her place this afternoon when I was there."

"You don't look too worried by his presence here."

Luc grinned. "I'm not. The guy's a loser. He stole some work of hers, then passed it off as his own. I thought it would be good for him to see that she's risen beyond that, so I invited him here."

"You did?" Gray raised his eyebrows. "Why?"

"So she'd face him, see that he can't hurt her anymore."

"You sound pretty confident. Anything you want to share?" Gray tilted back on the heels of his cowboy boots, obviously waiting.

Luc shrugged. "Well, I could tell you that I've entered into a three-way partnership with the Darlings."

"About time, too." Gray slapped him on the back. "Glad you finally decided to stay. What changed your mind?"

Luc jerked his head forward. "She did."

"Dani? I thought you said there was nothing between you."

"There isn't. Not yet. But there could be if she'd give it half a chance."

"Well, don't sound so mournful. It's not like you can't bide your time and wait for her."

"I could wait. But she won't. She says she's leaving town as soon as the play is over. Only don't let on I told you that, okay? She wants to tell you herself."

"All right."

Gray looked confused, but Luc had no time to illuminate him. Dani had called for rehearsal to begin. He made sure his trench coat was buttoned, tilted his fedora to a jaunty angle as she'd instructed, and waited for his cue.

A flash halted his progress on stage and Luc glanced up, scanning the hall for the source. Brad Conway held a video recorder to his eye. He was taping Dani's play!

"Can we try that again, please? Luc, pay attention."

He had to tell her, but not now. He'd tell her later, after rehearsal was over. He'd catch her alone, warn her. If Brad was true to form, he would try to steal this one, too. And it would be Luc's fault for inviting him here.

But the night dragged on as they discussed several problems with costumes, the set, and timing. He waited, but Dani was busy. It wasn't the time to interrupt.

As he listened to the others bring up a myriad of problems, Luc realized that tonight he'd finally lost his nervousness. Not completely, just enough so that he could say the words clearly, give them emphasis without stumbling over them. He could keep his place; he recognized when he should come in.

As triumphs went, it wasn't a bad one at all. And it proved that Dani was good for him, that he needed her with him.

"Luc?" Winifred stood beside him, a quizzical look on her face. "I just heard Dani tell Marissa McGonigle that she wouldn't be doing this again. Is something wrong? Is directing the play, the dinner theater—is it too much, after her illness and everything?" She looked troubled as she studied their young leader.

"She's fine, Miss Win. Maybe a bit tired, but she'll come back quickly enough. That's one thing about the young, they recover fast." He glanced down. "But what about you? Is this whole meal thing too much? I don't want you to keel over."

She glared at him. "I'm not going to 'keel over,'

Lucas. I never keel over. I have everything under control. The food is all parceled out to be cooked in various locations. Except for the vegetables. I'll do those here. And the meat. We'll carve that here.''

She rattled on about her plans for serving the meal. It sounded to Luc as if she did indeed have the preparation streamlined.

"Then, what's bothering you?"

Winifred Blessing didn't answer right away. He followed her glance to Dani, who sat among a group of people, her head nodding now and then, but it was clear she wasn't concentrating. In fact, she offered no suggestions, but let the group form a consensus as to their actions, then noted their decision in her book.

"It's as if she's stepped back, opted out. I can't explain it, really. It's just a feeling I have."

Luc knew she was concerned. Winifred loved Dani as if she were her own niece. She'd cared for her, pitched in for the dinner theater, advised her. Luc couldn't hold back the truth.

"She's leaving as soon as the play is finished," he said. "She doesn't want anyone to know, but that's her plan." He explained about Dermot's notation in the diaries.

"Fancy Dancer." Miss Winifred tapped one fingernail against her forehead. "I know that name. But I cannot think why. Was it a horse Dermot used to have?"

"We don't know. We may never know. The result is that Dani believes she has to pay Gray for that land and she's determined to do it."

"Ah. I see. That explains the antiques. I did wonder why."

Luc shook his head in amazement. Miss Winifred was clearly faster at working this stuff out than he.

"You're going to just stand back and let her go?" Her blue eyes were dark with hidden emotion. "I thought she meant more to you."

"She means everything! But she won't give me a chance—us a chance. She's afraid."

"I know."

The softly spoken words surprised him.

"I sensed it when she first came back. It was as if she'd run home to hide, but then she had to deal with Dermot's death. She's been retreating ever since. But I had such hopes—" She turned, pinned him with her eyes. "Don't you have a plan?"

"Sort of." He met her stare with a sheepish smile. "It's nothing grand, nothing too elaborate. Just an idea I have."

To his surprise, Miss Win didn't pry or ask any questions about his intentions. She simply nodded, patted him on the arm.

"You work on your plan, dear," she said, but her gaze was on Dani. "I think I'll work on mine." She scanned the room as if searching for something. "Excuse me, I have an errand to run."

Luc watched as she scurried across the room and out the door.

"What's she up to?" Gray asked, rubbing his shoulder.

"I have no idea. Are you sure we shouldn't have x-rayed that shoulder along with your brother's back? Maybe you tore something."

"That's what I said." Marissa McGonigle tilted an eyebrow at her husband. "But you know cowboys, Luc. Never take the easy way out. My hero would rather be brave and suffer in silence." She looped her arm through his. "Come on, honey. Cody's already out cold. It's time to get you both home."

"Yeah. I guess you're right." Gray winked at Luc over one shoulder. "A back rub sure would be nice. Maybe after we tuck Cody in you could use some of that oil you bought in Denver last Christmas. Seemed to do the trick then."

"Shh! Be quiet, Gray. The whole town doesn't need to hear about your love of lavender." Marissa glanced back at Luc, her cheeks red as fire. But there was a gleam in her eyes that Luc envied as he watched them gather up their son and disappear into the darkness.

He wanted that for himself. Ached for that invisible bond between two people that didn't require words to say the things that were most important. He wanted the right to take Dani's hand and steal away to a place where no one else could go, where whatever happened in the past didn't matter, where they could plan and dream of a future they would share.

Please, God, let me have that chance.

"You're sure this is what you want to do?"

"It's what I have to do," Dani replied, but she didn't look at him. She sensed he was about to protest and held up one hand. "Can we not go over this again? Please? Can you just help me?"

Silence yawned between them. She knew what he was thinking about tomorrow, opening night. By Saturday evening they'd know whether or not the dinner theater was a success, whether they'd achieved their goal.

What Luc didn't know was that on Sunday she'd be gone. Her heart yearned to wipe away his pain, to stay here, accept what he offered. But the acorn of distrust wouldn't be dislodged. If he let her down, if she banked everything on her feelings and she was wrong again—

No! She couldn't. She had to go it alone.

Luc might still hope for a reprieve, but Dani knew what she had to do.

"Yes, I'll help you, Dani." The words were quiet, solemn and totally sincere. "Always."

She turned, stared at him, willing her brain to try, to trust him a little, to hope. But the voice would not be silenced.

Sooner or later he'd let you down, Dani. Everyone has. Your father, your mother, Brad, even your professors when they didn't recognize your work. Try as hard as he will, Luc will do the same. You can't trust anyone. You have to depend on yourself.

In the echoes of her mind she heard her father's voice from long ago: *"Learn to stand on your own two feet, girl. It's all right to ask for help if there's no other way, but, honey, there's always another way. You just have to find it. A DeWitt doesn't need anybody. A DeWitt stands alone."*

With all her heart, Dani hoped Dermot was right, because at this precise moment, the thought of never seeing Luc again, never hearing that slow drawl of his when he teased her, never feeling his hand against her cheek—it all seemed too much to give up.

"You're sure this is what you want?"

The softly voiced question slammed the reality of her situation home.

"Yes." She climbed into his passenger seat, fastened her seat belt and waited for him to start down the road to Gray's. "By the way, I hear congratulations are in order, partner."

He nodded, glanced at her, then returned his attention to the road. "Yes. I'm officially one-third owner of Blessing Medical Group." His fingers tightened on the wheel for a moment, then he looked at her. "If you ever need me, Dani, if you ever want me to come and get you, for any reason, this is where I'll be. Right here in Blessing. Waiting for you to come home."

"Please don't." Tears filled her eyes and she turned to stare out the window. A minute later his fingers curled over hers, and because it was so good to feel his touch, she retained the contact.

Luc said nothing more, and twenty minutes later they pulled into Gray's yard. Cody was chasing the dog around the yard and he paused just long enough to wave before he again raced after the golden collie, little legs churning.

Dani got out of the car, then realized that Luc was still sitting inside, staring after the boy. She leaned down.

"Luc?"

"Yeah?" He jerked to awareness, then grinned and got out of the truck. "I was just imagining what it would be like to have a couple like him running around."

Dani froze, her heart squeezing into a tight round ball of pure, unadulterated pain as she pictured two little boys, mud-spattered but happy, staring up at their father with big brown eyes so like Luc's. She blinked—and the vision wavered and was gone, leaving an empty ache behind.

If only she could leave today, get in the old truck and drive until the anguish stopped.

The front door opened. Gray stepped onto the porch.

"Luc?" He took the steps two at a time, then slowed when he saw her. "Dani. Is anything wrong?"

Luc stayed where he was, waiting for her to take the first step that would send her away.

"Nothing's wrong, Gray. But I need to talk to you. Is now okay?"

"Sure. Marissa just made some coffee. Your timing is perfect." He glanced over at Cody.

Dani saw the glint of pride flash through Gray's eyes as Cody clambered onto the top rail of a fence and seated himself there, intent on watching the horse that had injured Adam.

"You stay out of there, Cody. It's dangerous."

Cody nodded. "I'll be careful, Dad. Promise."

Gray scanned the yard, then nodded. His gaze returned to Dani, a question hovering in the steely depths of his eyes. "Come on in."

"Dani! It's been ages since you were over." Marissa hugged her, then Luc, then ordered them to the table. "I just took this out of the oven. Maybe we'll actually get to taste it before Gray eats it all." She giggled when he pinched her cheek. "Well, you are rather partial to pineapple upside-down cake."

"Hate the stuff," Gray whispered loudly as he sat down. "I just eat it to keep her happy."

They shared a look that made Dani's knees weaken. She accepted her mug of coffee and hung onto it to keep from reaching out for Luc.

"So what brings you by?"

"I've got some problems, Gray." She searched for the right way to phrase it.

"It happens. Ranching isn't like it was." He cut into his cake, rolled his eyes and groaned. "Man, this is good. You keep this up, Rissa, and I'll be three hundred pounds before I reach forty.''

"When you are, come and see me. I just read about this new diet and I'm dying to try it on one of my patients. You eat cabbage soup for six days and fast on the seventh.'' Luc winked at Dani, but his face was bland when he met Gray's disgusted look.

"I'll cut down on my own, thanks,'' the big rancher muttered, scooping up the last bite on his plate. He waved away Marissa's second helping. "No thanks. The thought of six days' worth of cabbage soup is threat enough.''

His wife giggled when Luc helped himself to that second slice.

"So you were saying?'' Gray tore his gaze from the golden cake and turned to Dani.

Dani shifted, uncomfortable with the intense scrutiny. She decided to just get it over with.

"I found some old entries in my father's diary about a horse called Fancy Dancer. Have you heard of it?''

Gray shook his head, his forehead furrowed. "Doesn't sound familiar. Is it important?''

"I think so. Dad wrote that he gave your father this horse in trade for some land—the river section.'' She saw the concern flood his face. "I know. It doesn't make sense. There's no way one horse, one unknown horse, could have been valuable enough to cover the cost of that land. Not even back then.''

"Maybe he wasn't unknown.''

Dani shook her head. "I've researched this pretty thoroughly. There's no horse by that name listed in any of the big races, no records of bloodline. Nothing.''

"I see.''

Luc's hand moved under the cover of the table to

grasp hers and offer a squeeze of encouragement. His touch helped her relax a little. She went on.

"So unless you have some record of the transaction, I have to assume that Dad gave the horse to Harris as some kind of down payment. I want to clean up my father's affairs, so I'm hoping you'll accept this as the balance of payment for that land." She set the stack of bills on the table.

Gray gaped. "But you hold title, don't you?"

"Yes, and I'd like to keep it. But I can't do that knowing that this debt was never paid off." There, she'd gotten through the worst of it. Now if she could just get him to agree to the rest. "I know I'll still owe the interest for all this time. I was hoping that maybe you'd want to rent the Double D for Adam and apply that rent to the interest."

Gray shook his head, reached out and shoved the money back toward her. "Dani, I can't take this. We don't know what happened all those years ago. Your father wouldn't have cheated mine—" He stopped, eyes widening.

"You're remembering the argument." She nodded. "It was before my time, but it must have been something pretty major to keep them angry at each other for all those years. I think they argued about my father's nonpayment."

"Maybe. But—"

"I have to do this, Gray. If someday we find out I'm wrong, we'll deal with it then." She leaned toward him, trying to make him understand. "I don't want to lose the Double D, but I can't run it, either. You of all people know that."

"You need help, that's all."

She shook her head, energy dissipated, hopes disintegrating. "All the help in the world wouldn't make me the rancher my father was. I've tried, but I just can't do it anymore. Please, please do this. I need to have my conscience clear." She glanced at Marissa for help, but the woman was staring at the wall, her attention obviously elsewhere.

"Gray, ever since I came back there's been a kind of wall between us. Probably because of our fathers' problems, I don't know. What I do know is that you've been a real friend to me lately when I needed it most. I'm asking you to be my friend now. If you can possibly swing it, do this one last thing."

"Last?" He looked from her to Luc in puzzled surprise. "If Adam's running your spread, where will you be?"

"Doing something else. My plans aren't entirely certain yet." She deliberately didn't say more, in spite of Luc's frown and the pressure of his fingers. "I just know I have to get the ranch settled before I can move on."

Gray studied her for a long time before he looked at Luc. Then his eyes moved to the stack of bills she'd laid there. "Well, I've never seen so much cash at once," he frowned. "Why did you—?"

"Everyone in town has been speculating about the Double D and its debts for months. Daddy would have expected me to handle this on my own. I wanted our transaction to be private, just between us. The past isn't anyone else's business. That's why I got cash." She held her breath, waiting.

"If you're sure this is what you want, I'll agree. But the money goes into a special account. If you learn anything—and I mean *anything*—different, you get it back. All of it. Deal?" He held out a hand.

"Deal." Dani unthreaded her fingers from Luc's and lifted her hand to meet his. "And thank you."

"I should be thanking you. That brother of mine needs something to ground him. The Double D just might be the answer, though there's no way he's going to be able to handle it for a while. He's cut up pretty bad."

"I have just one thing more to ask of you." She saw the way his eyes flared, saw the concern grow. "I don't want Adam to alter the river section. I want it left alone. It was Daddy's favorite, and if I ever come back, I'll want it wild and rugged, just as it is."

Gray's glance flashed to Luc. Dani felt Luc shift beside her, but before she could turn his way, Gray was speaking.

"No problem. Adam's not exactly into roughing it, anyway. And there's nothing back there but a few deer. He won't touch it."

"Thank you." Dani rose. "I'd better get going. I've got a lot of things to do before tomorrow night."

"You've done a great job with that play, Dani." Marissa stood beside Gray. "It's funny, yet so touching. There must be a producer somewhere that would kill to show that on Broadway. Who wrote it, anyhow? Anyone we know?"

"Dani wrote it."

Luc ignored the darts she threw with her eyes as he told her secret.

"She didn't want anyone to know, but I think credit should go where it's due." He brushed his knuckles against her cheek. "I know I promised not to say it, but Gray and Marissa are friends. They respect what you've created. So would the rest of the town, if you'd just tell them."

"I'd rather you not tell anyone, at least until it's over." By then it wouldn't matter. She'd be long gone and the whole town of Blessing could speculate on whether or not the sad little female character in the play was based on Dani's own life experiences or not.

"But everyone would be so proud—" Gray stopped as Marissa's elbow nudged his side.

Dani supposed she should have known Luc would tell. He wasn't ashamed of his past. He didn't have to hide behind silly excuses. He was open and honest and he trusted everyone. Unlike her.

"We won't tell anyone, Dani. Not if you don't want us to. But it is very, very good." Marissa smiled.

"Thanks." Dani breathed a bit easier. "And thanks for helping me out. Maybe I should have told you earlier, but I wanted to get as many facts about this Fancy Dancer thing as I could. I based the price of the land on what pieces the same size were selling for around here years ago. If you don't think it's right—"

"It's fine. Now I'm going to ask one thing of you, Dani."

Gray's piercing stare seemed to see through her barriers.

"What is that?" She forced her body not to flinch as she waited.

Gray's wry smile flickered over his face, causing the dimple at the side of his mouth to dance.

"Can you once and for all, forget about that land and debts and all the rest and just feel free to call on me if you need help? Can you do that?"

He was sincere, she decided after studying him for several minutes. His eyes shone a pure clear gray that held no ulterior motives. Dani nodded.

"Yes," she agreed.

Dani and Luc said their farewells, then walked to the car. Marissa and Gray stood on the porch, waved. Luc seated Dani inside, then climbed into the car himself.

"There now, that wasn't so hard. Was it?"

"No. I guess not." The air was chilly, the wind brisk as it whistled through the open window. "Oh, I forgot my sweater. I'll just run and get it. I won't be a minute."

Before he could answer, Dani was out of the car and across the yard. Her sweater hung on the coat hook just inside the screen door. She lifted a hand to knock, then froze.

"I'm telling you, Gray, I know that name, Fancy Dancer. I just can't remember why I know it. It's tucked away in a corner of my mind right now, but eventually I'll remember."

"Does it matter what happened in the past? Dad always claimed Dermot owed him. I just never knew why. And I'm glad. I'd like to let it die. There's no reason Dani should have to shoulder a debt that old."

"But she did." Marissa sounded thoughtful. "I just wish I could remember, but all I get is this vague recollection that your father got angry at that name, Fancy Dancer. I wonder if the horse was a dud?"

"Who cares?" Gray threaded an arm around her waist and drew her against him. "Haven't you got better things to think about?"

"Like what?" She lifted her hands to his shoulders and smiled at him.

"Like me."

They were so wrapped up in each other, they didn't even notice when Dani reached in and snatched her sweater. She walked back to the car, heart heavy as she mused on the obvious devotion the couple shared.

If only—

"You got it, I see." Luc waited while she belted up, then started the engine. "I'm proud of you," he said. "That had to be tough." He leaned over, brushed his lips against her cheek.

It wasn't hard at all compared to what she'd have to go through on Saturday night when she let Lucas Lawrence walk out of her life. Dani wanted so badly to turn and throw herself into his arms, to let him shoulder her burdens, to sink into the warmth of love he offered so unstintingly. But she couldn't.

It was easy to tell Gray she'd trust him. She was leaving town, the need would never arise. But to trust Luc, to let him into her deepest soul, to love him so completely that she'd trust him never to betray her— that was not to be.

If she'd needed proof, she'd had it tonight when he told her secret about authoring the play. A small betrayal, perhaps, one in which he'd thought he was helping her. But wasn't that how it always began?

Luc wouldn't see it that way. He'd say he wanted to share her gift with others, to make them part of her success. But Dani needed to preserve that mask.

Because if he saw beneath it, he would see how truly unlovable she was—that she deserved to be betrayed because she wasn't worth loving.

Chapter Thirteen

"Well? What do you think?" Luc's fingers wove through hers naturally as he led her slowly up the pathway to the building where their dinner theater would be held.

Tiny white fairy lights twinkled in a continuous arbor overhead while small white paper bags with candles flickering inside marked the edges of the walk. To the left and right of the hall, picnic tables were arranged in small open spots, and here too, candles shone. Black-suited wait staff appeared here and there bearing trays filled with sparkling glasses of something gold and shimmering.

"It's fantastic," she breathed, enthralled by the effort someone had gone to. "Who did this?"

"Nicole and Joshua."

The couple stood alongside Marissa and Gray, at the doorway into the hall, greeting those who arrived, taking their tickets and showing them their places.

"We're sold out tonight," Nicole told her. "And tomorrow night. There are three tickets left for Saturday, but I don't think they'll last long.''

''You've done a wonderful job with the grounds—'' Dani interrupted herself to gasp at her first glimpse of the hall she'd left in turmoil this afternoon. Satisfied with her reaction, the couples grinned, then happily returned to their arriving guests.

The plain hall had been transformed into a clearing in the middle of the deep forest. Evergreens in fat buckets lined the walls, their boughs swaying gently overhead. Tiny lights flickered above like a thousand stars. Their light provided a romantic shadowy glow. Scattered throughout the hall were round tables dressed in floor-length white cloths. Each table held a white pillar candle perched upon a tuft of gold tulle that protected the candle from the rough edges of a black wrought-iron holder. A tiny black bow tie was wrapped around the evening's program, marking each place setting.

''It looks like something from *A Midsummer Night's Dream*,'' she whispered, standing on tiptoe to reach Luc's ear. ''It's perfect. Far beyond what I expected.''

Though the room offered a tantalizing aroma of what was to come, and though Dani knew Miss Winifred and her crew were busily working their magic in the kitchen, no sound of dishes penetrated the soft, melodic strains of a pan flute that wavered around the room.

Overwhelmed by her dream come to life, Dani turned to Luc, wrapped her arms around him and hugged for all she was worth to hide the tears that filled her eyes.

He laughed and hugged her back.

''I take it you like it.'' He leaned back, grinned, eyes crinkling at the corners.

In the soft light even Luc seemed mysterious, almost a stranger.

"It's exactly what I dreamed of," she murmured, her fingers touching the strands that lay against the nape of his neck, needing to reassure herself that he hadn't changed. His tailored black suit and pristine white shirt had altered him from the comfortable friend she knew to an elegant stranger. But when she looked into his eyes, she knew it was Luc. The warmth lay there, lambent, welcoming. "You look very handsome."

"Thank you." His arms tightened. "You fit here, Dani."

She could have stayed forever like that, surrounded by his arms, safe against his broad chest, staring into that haven of peace she always found in his eyes. If only…

"Stay."

Dismayed by the intensity in his tone, she searched his face, saw only love.

"Luc, I—"

"Please stay."

Yes, her heart answered. But as she looked around, caught the curious glances directed their way, she knew that staying was impossible. Life wasn't made up of moments like this, however much she wished it were.

"Luc, I…um…"

"You two are a sight for sore eyes." Miss Winifred stood two feet away. "Not that mine are. Sore, I mean." She chuckled at her own foolishness. "I can't tell you how excited I am, Dani. Not only are we raising much-needed money for a good cause, but we're having so much fun doing it. Furly's kept us in stitches for the past half hour."

Dani let her arms drop from Luc's neck, sad that the moment had been broken, but also relieved that she hadn't given herself away. Luc left one arm loosely around her waist, as if it belonged there.

"Is everything okay in the kitchen?" she whispered, praying nothing would spoil the hard work of so many people.

"Everything is perfect. We're right on time. Are your actors all here?"

Dani jerked to awareness. "Actors. Good grief, I almost forgot. Come on, Luc." She glanced at her watch. "We've only got half an hour before curtain time."

"Everyone's ready. There's no need to rush." But he walked beside her to the side door that led to the stage, opened it, waited for her to pass through. Once they were inside, alone, he stopped. "You look very lovely, Dani."

She paused at the bottom of the stairs. "Thank you. And I don't mean just for the compliment. I don't know how you did it, but the decorations, the setting, it's all absolutely perfect. I never imagined that when you ordered me to go home this afternoon you had all this planned."

"It wasn't just me. Big Ed's been into making this a stellar production from the start. Along with a lot of others." He lifted one hand, brushed a tendril away from her mouth, his smile sad. "You can trust us, Dani. I've told you that over and over. We're on your side. But I guess you're one of those people who has to see it to believe it."

"I didn't mean—"

He lifted the hand he held to his mouth, kissed her palm. "I know," he whispered. "I love you. And I'm still praying."

The hope in those words took her breath away.

"Oh, Luc." Tears welled. "I wish it could be different. You're such a wonderful man. But I can't stay here. I can't.''

He studied her for a long time, until a noise on stage drew their attention.

''Come on, sweetheart. We've got a show to put on.''

She preceded him up the stairs, the endearment ringing in her ears. He'd said it so naturally. It seemed good, right. And yet she couldn't say it back.

You've stolen my peace, Luc. You pushed your way into my life and my heart in a way no other person ever has. I don't know how to deal with that. I want to trust. I want so badly to trust. But I'm afraid.

It wasn't that she didn't love him. She'd loved him for weeks, even months. It had grown slowly, found a corner of her heart and nestled there, growing, until now, even when she was completely involved in something else, her mind would suddenly fly to him, wonder what he was doing, if he was thinking of her.

She'd be out riding, the wind chafing her cheeks, and suddenly she would feel a deep, intense longing to know that someone waited for her, someone who would always be there, someone who would fill her heart and soul, and she would clench her teeth against the pain. That someone of her dreams was always Luc.

God, please help me. Please help me do the right thing. Don't let me hurt him. Teach me how to live without Luc.

''Dani?'' The pressure of his fingers on hers brought her back to the present.

''I'm fine. Go do your stuff.'' She watched him walk away, steeled herself against the hurt.

Actors scurried about backstage, checking each other's costumes, practicing lines, sipping water to keep their throats lubricated. Dani stayed in the shadows and watched, her eyes returning again and again to Luc. For a man who couldn't speak in public, Luc seemed remarkably calm. He teased and joked, even conveyed a sense of composure that calmed the actors. The voices softened, the questions became less frantic. Finally they gathered in a circle.

Luc scanned the area, found her and beckoned.

When she joined him, he said, "We want to pray together, just the cast and you, before we begin."

She nodded, bowed her head and waited. After a minute, it became clear that they expected her to lead them. Dani was so nervous she was afraid her voice would fail, but she took a deep breath, concentrated on the person she was speaking to, and dove in.

"Father, this is Your night, not ours. We began this project to raise money for the orphanage, but we know that You can use our efforts in many ways. We ask You to help us now, give us clear speech, perfect memories. Be with those who labor with the meal, the serving, the doors, the lights and all the other things. But one thing we ask above all, keep us focused on You, God, the true author and finisher of our play. Amen."

She raised her head, found Luc watching her and smiled. She felt the love emanating from him and drew on it to bolster her courage.

"You've all studied, practiced, rehearsed and prayed. Now it's time to do it. God bless." The others repeated the phrase, eyes shining. "All right. Places, please."

She knew Big Ed had already checked the sound system, that their guests were seated, that the lights were ready. Dani tucked her purse into a hidden corner, patted her hair and drew a deep breath. Then she walked to the center of the stage and nodded for the curtains to be drawn.

"Ladies and gentlemen, we welcome you. Our presentation tonight will be in three acts. Between those acts, your meal will be served. If you require anything, we ask that you simply blow out the candle on your table and your server will assist you. Now we invite you to sit back, relax, and enjoy our performance of *Three-Dollar Dreams.*"

She stepped back and the curtain whooshed closed as applause filled the hall.

"Act one, scene one. Places please. Ready?" She glanced around at the cast, saw their trusting faces and realized that all involved in this production had put their faith in her.

No one had asked if she had the knowledge, the capability, the experience to do this. No one had questioned her directions, told her they were disappointed in her leadership, or asked her to rework the play. No one had suggested that the project was too difficult, too demanding or too hard to achieve.

Why was that?

Her eyes rested on Luc as he stood in the wings, waiting to enter the stage as soon as the curtain was drawn. He smiled at her and she knew the answer.

They'd trusted her.

Now it was time for her to trust them.

"We're ready, Dani. We can do this." She couldn't see the actor nor identify the speaker. But the assurance in that voice encouraged her.

She smiled back, her heart in her throat. "Yes," she whispered. "I know you can."

She motioned for the curtain to open.

Chapter Fourteen

The last day.

The last night.

Dani deliberately took her time preparing for the last performance, indulging in the longest bubble bath she'd ever taken. Then she concentrated on her makeup, combing each curl, darkening each eyelash. It was imperative that she look her best tonight. She wouldn't let anyone down, she wouldn't let anyone see, no matter how hard it was to hide the truth. Just for tonight she would be Dani DeWitt, the carefree girl that everyone could count on.

Tomorrow she would leave Blessing. For good.

She'd been to the hall earlier, checked every microphone, every spotlight, every costume. Everything was in order. Everything was taken care of.

She had pulled into the parking lot a scant five minutes before curtain time. Now she stepped inside, scanned the hall. Every seat was filled.

"We thought something had happened. Luc's been frantic." Gray put her arm in his and walked her to the side door. The teasing grin he used to flash at her long ago, when they'd shared the bus to school, appeared as he squeezed her arm. "The guy loves you, Dani. Cut him some slack."

She smiled but said nothing. Inside the darkened alley, she drew three deep breaths, whispered a prayer for help, then climbed the stairs. The actors sat in a circle on the floor. Luc stood to one side.

"She'll be here. We just have to trust that she'll be here."

"I'm here."

They turned, stared at her, then grinned. Luc practically raced across the stage, swooped her into his arms and, mindless of their audience, kissed her as if she'd been away a year. The entire troupe clapped.

"You scared me," he said, nuzzling her neck as he ignored them. "My knees are shaking."

"Why? I'm not a quitter. I intend to see this thing through." She eased herself carefully away, not wanting to hurt him, but afraid he'd see the longing in her eyes and know the truth. She allowed one hand to trail down his cheek. "You'd better wipe off that lipstick, Inspector." She glanced around. "Millicent, your skirt isn't right. Where's Ephraim? I want him to check that microphone."

The few problems she could find resolved themselves in seconds. A hush fell over the cast.

"This is our final night. I want to tell you how proud I am of each of you. It looks as if we've raised the entire amount the orphanage needs."

A quiet cheer.

"Now let's give these people their money's worth." As she'd done each night, Dani led them in a prayer, then offered her last words of advice. "Make it shine, people. Make it shine."

She took her place center stage and waited. When all was quiet, she nodded at Big Ed.

Wanting to savor the moment just a second longer, Dani scanned the crowd. Her body froze when her gaze landed on a man with a video camera at the farthest table. Brad Conway had his lens focused directly on her.

"Dani?"

Luc's whisper reminded her of her duty. She tore her eyes from her betrayer, concentrated on her job, on their dinner guests, on anything but Brad.

"So sit back, relax, and enjoy our final performance of *Three-Dollar Dreams*."

Moments later, Luc strode on stage, his voice strong and resonant. The entire first act went without a hitch, every member coming in at the correct time, not a line forgotten. But Dani couldn't get her focus off the man in the audience with the camera. When the curtain fell on act one, she cornered Luc.

"What is Brad Conway doing here?" she demanded.

"He bought the last three tickets this afternoon. He and some friends of his—from New York, I think— wanted to see your work." Luc unbuttoned his coat, took several deep breaths. "Next time you write a play, don't put the guy in a trench coat," he muttered. "I'm burning up."

"You'll be lucky if I don't set you on fire." Dani didn't smile, she couldn't. Her mind was too busy trying to grapple with his words. She couldn't believe he'd done it. "How could you let Brad come here, film everything? You know what he did to me. And now you've set it up to happen again!"

Bitterness rolled over her like waves as she imagined

her sad story plastered across Broadway. That hurt far more than knowing Brad's name would be featured underneath.

"I thought I could trust you," she whispered. "I thought you, of all people, knew what this play means to me. I thought you'd understand—"

Understand what? That in the play she'd bared her soul, told the whole world of the pain that filled her heart? Did she actually hope Luc might see past the jokes and the cute phrases, know how desperately she wanted to find the one place in this world where she truly belonged, the one person she could depend on forever?

She expected him to understand all of that from acting in a silly play? How foolish to hope that Luc was the person she could lean on. *Wrong again,* her brain chirped.

She saw Luc frown, heard him say something. But she couldn't stay to listen. She turned and strode away from him, out the side door and into the dusk where she could hide from all of them.

She lingered in the shelter of a big ponderosa pine and let the crisp evening air cool her burning cheeks and dry her tears until the last possible moment. Then she slipped into her place in the wings, ready to prompt at the least sign of faltering.

Luc stood waiting for the curtain to open. He scanned the area, found her and stared, his face solemn, a touch of sadness lingering at the edges of his mouth as his eyes searched hers. Then the curtain whooshed open and act two began.

The performance was flawless, honed to perfection. Sensitive to the timing of each word, they performed as professionals, drawing every emotion from their crowd.

When the curtain fell on the last act, the silence was deafening, and for a moment Dani's heart stopped. Then came a burst of applause and the entire hall erupted in calls of "Bravo!"

As instructed, the actors lined up across the stage, arms entwined, waited for the curtain to lift, then bowed. Once. Twice. Then Luc walked over, drew her out of the shadows and to the center of the stage. The applause grew louder.

Tears rolled down her cheeks—happiness mingled with sadness. She nodded, spread her hands to the actors and applauded them, then motioned for Winifred to come forward and thanked her. The clapping never ceased. She motioned for the curtain to go down, but Luc stepped forward, announced her as author of the play, and laid a sheaf of bloodred roses in her arms. Then he kissed her.

"Thank you, Dani," he whispered, then stepped back into the troupe's line, applauding her with the rest.

She didn't know what to do. The emotions wouldn't be held in check as she moved down the row, congratulating each one. Finally the curtain dropped.

Luc stood before her. The others melted away.

"I need to talk to you, Dani. I want to explain." His fingers trapped her arm, preventing escape. "You don't understand."

"Sure I do." She dredged up a smile. "The play's over now. There's nothing more to talk about. You did a wonderful job. Thank you." She tugged her arm out of his grasp and turned away. "Excuse me, please. There are some things I need to do."

Pain ricocheted through her, and a longing so fierce it threatened to swamp her, as Dani turned and walked away from the man she'd trusted with everything. She stuffed her feelings down, concentrated on ensuring the hall was restored to its former order, burying herself in the myriad of details she'd handed off weeks ago.

She had stepped outside the door for a breath of air, when a hand on her arm stopped her.

"Dani? Could I speak to you? Please?"

She looked up into Brad's face and every nerve zinged to attention.

"I don't think so, Brad," she managed to say with dignity. "We don't really have anything to talk about, do we?" She turned away, but his voice stopped her.

"We could, if you'd just listen for a minute."

She turned her head, smiled at him. "Maybe some other time. Good night."

Brad didn't move, so Dani did. She hurried away into the kitchen and found Miss Winifred busily packing. Dani helped her carry out the supplies she'd brought from the bakery, waited as each item was stored inside the van. Then Winifred turned to her, her face beaming.

"My dear, I can't tell you how proud I was to be a part of this. Not only did we raise the funds we needed, but also we've impacted the lives of everyone who saw your play. You may never know how many lives you touched here, Dani."

"Thank you. But we couldn't have done it without you, Miss Win. I appreciate everything you did." She wanted to run, to get away to some private place and bawl her eyes out. But she held it together. Just a few moments longer, she told herself.

"Yes, well…" Miss Winifred stared into her eyes and frowned. She opened her mouth to add something more, but Dani interrupted.

"I'd better get home. Good night."

"Good night, dear. Rest well." Miss Winifred hugged her, then let her go.

Dani strode to her car, climbed inside and started the engine. Big Ed was in charge of locking up and she'd let him do his job without interference. On the way out of the parking lot, she caught sight of Luc's tall lean form as he stood under a light stand, hands gesturing, talking to someone. Brad. They were deep in conversation.

Traitor. She stepped on the gas.

Luc glanced up, noticed her, moved forward, but she roared past, pretending she hadn't seen him.

The evening was clear, the moon full as it lit the way to the ranch. She drove slowly, absorbing each detail, reminded of the places she'd grown up.

"Why?" she whispered, blinking away the tears. "Why bring me back just to take it all away? Why are You doing this?"

I know the plans I have for you. The scripture verse came to her in bits.

"I don't. What plans are they?" The questions rose up in a tide of frustration.

Plans to prosper you, not to hurt you.

"How does leaving my home prosper me?" she demanded, irritated that the one time God spoke to her heart, she couldn't understand.

Is leaving my plan? Or is it His?

The question shocked her. Her plan? What did that mean? That she wanted to leave? That she wasn't obeying? She turned right automatically, headed down the dusty road toward the Double D.

"Please tell me Your plan. Or show me where I've gone wrong."

A deep searching darkness seemed to settle on the car. *Do I love God?*

Love God? Of course she did, had since she'd known He was there.

Then why don't I trust Him?

She pulled to a halt in front of the house, her mind searching to understand.

Do I trust that God is love? That He wants to give me my heart's desire?

Love was so hard to understand—a father's love especially so. Her father had loved her, she'd always known that. But he wasn't inclined to displays of affection, he seldom showed his love in physical ways.

But God wasn't like Dermot. God loved her more than her father could.

More than Daddy? She considered that. She stepped out of the car, then let herself into the house, her mind trying to conceive of such a love.

Dani automatically stepped out of her fancy dress, slipped on a sweatshirt and a pair of jeans, her mind busy sorting through this puzzle. She made herself a cup of hot peppermint tea, snatched up her Bible and went to sit on the veranda. She needed to understand this, needed to hear whatever God was trying to say. Mostly she needed answers.

She sipped her tea thoughtfully, paging through her Bible as she searched. Her hand paused above a notation she'd made in a margin.

"God's blessings are dispensed according to the riches of His grace, not according to the depth of our faith."

The Scripture passage following made her eyes open wide.

"If we are not faithful, He will still be faithful, because He cannot be false to Himself."

She frowned. So God was telling her that He'd done His part? That she was the one giving up?

She fingered the bookmark, flipped the thin onionskin pages backward. The verse, clearly visible in the center of the page, hit her heart.

"Without faith, no one can please God. Anyone who comes to God must believe that He is real and that He rewards those who truly want to find Him."

Without faith... Her eyes burned as Dani faced the truth.

She hadn't practiced faith in her recent relationship with God. She'd merely assessed the situation and assumed God was punishing her. But what about trust? What about giving up the need to control everything and everyone, and depending on her heavenly Father to make things turn out right?

Luc's face swam before her, his eyes troubled as he listened to her angry denunciation tonight. What had he been trying to say? Why was it so hard to listen to him, to accept the love he offered?

Because she didn't trust him, just as she didn't trust God. She couldn't. Because trusting someone else meant you gave up the controls, you surrendered your hand on the rudder because you believed in someone else, trusted that they wouldn't fail you.

Except, they would. She remembered her father and the truth hit her squarely. People would always fail each other. Not because they wanted to, not because they meant to. But humans failed.

But God didn't. He never failed to do exactly as He promised. He was the one rock she could always count on. If she would only give in and let Him be in charge.

The truth filled her, lighting up the dark corners of her mind, offering hope for a future security that could not be shaken. Why hadn't she seen it before? Why hadn't she relied on the One whose arms were always there? She'd been afraid to accept Luc's love because some part of her brain understood that she was placing her faith in the wrong place.

Dani bowed her head.

"Father, I've been so wrong. I've hung on, refusing to let go and trust in You with each problem. If I'm in trouble now, it's not because of You, but because I didn't trust You to show me the way. Forgive me, Lord. You are the one in charge. I give the controls of my life back to You, where they belong. Show me the way I should go."

Around her the night air hung still, silent. Waiting.

"I trust You, God. Whatever You want. If You want me to leave Blessing, I will. And I'll look forward to the future You give. But if I could stay, Father... If I could have another chance—"

Dani swallowed the words. It was too late for her and Luc. In her heart she knew that. Now it was up to her to show her Lord that she would willingly wait to see what He would do, where He would lead.

"I am yours, Lord. Whatever You want."

She lifted her face into the soft caress of evening air, heart aching but open to receive from the Father's hand. And tenderly, the inner glow flickered to life and warmed her until she knew again the blessing of heaven's kiss.

It would be enough.

Sometime later she gathered up her things, prepared to go inside. Dani had no idea how long she'd sat there. Her tea was cold, the night cooler. She opened the door.

A *boom* reverberated through the valley, echoing over mountain and vale in a series of staccato bursts. She set down her things and moved to the side of the house, trying to identify the source of the noise. A shower of golden stars burst overhead and flickered brightly, lighting up the valley for a few precious seconds, before they tumbled to earth in a lavish display of fireworks.

Dani peered into the light, thought she glimpsed someone running. A rustler? But she had no cattle left, and anyway, a rustler wouldn't announce his presence with fireworks.

Another *crack* rang through the air. This time there was a *pop,* then three green arcs shimmered against the dark sky. She waited for more. Nothing. Then she thought she saw the flicker of fire.

She raced toward the barn, saddled Duke and set off across the land, intent on discovering who was trespassing. She couldn't go fast, there wasn't enough light for that. But she nudged Duke into a quick walk until they came to the crest of a hill where one lonely figure sat on her boulder. Waiting.

For her?

"Hi, Dani."

"Luc?" She dismounted, stared at him. "It's almost midnight. What are you doing?"

"Trying to get your attention." He watched her walk toward him.

"Well, it worked. I'm here. I suspect half the county heard you." She felt awkward, didn't know what to do. Finally she decided to just stand there and wait for his explanation.

He slid off the boulder and took her hands, dropping the reins she had been clutching.

"I didn't betray you, Dani. I would never do that."

"I know." She left her hands where they were, smiled at him. "I shouldn't have said that. I was just—"

"Mad?" he offered, a grin turning up the corners of his mouth.

She nodded, embarrassed.

He reached up, smoothed back a tendril of her hair, his fingers lingering against her cheek.

"You can't go, Dani. Not now. I know I said I was leaving all of this up to God, but I can't just stand by and let you go without telling you that I think God's plan is for you to stay right here. With me."

"I do too," she whispered.

"I love you. I can't watch you walk away, knowing—" He stopped, frowned. "I must have been too close to that last zinger," he said. "My ears are fuzzy. I thought I heard you say—" He shook his head. "Never mind. I was trying to tell you something."

"You said you loved me." She waited, longing to hear the precious words again. She didn't deserve this, but Dani had a hunch God was about to give her the desire of her heart and she wanted to make sure she got *all* of it.

"I do love you. I've told you enough times. I didn't arrange for Brad to be there tonight, but I'm glad he was because—"

Dani laid a finger over his lips. "I don't want to hear about Brad, Luc. I couldn't care less about him or his friends right now."

"Oh?" He cocked his head, peering at her. "Why?"

"Because I think God just gave me a second chance and I don't want to blow it talking about Brad. Would you mind continuing?"

Luc searched her eyes as a slow grin slid from his glossy chocolate-brown eyes, pinched the dimples in his cheeks and spread his mouth wide.

"Not at all. You sure you're listening?"

She nodded.

"I love you, Dani DeWitt. I think you're the smartest, most creative, talented, beautiful, adorable, wonderful woman I've ever known. I'm too old for you and I don't deserve you, but none of that seems to matter anymore. I want to marry you. I want us to build a life, together, in Blessing. I want to have a family, God willing. I want to help on the ranch. I want to find out all the things God has to teach me. And I want you right beside me until the last day I spend on earth. Is that doable?"

Dani could only stare as her heart offered silent praise to the God who loved her enough to send her a man like Luc.

"If you need a minute to consider my offer, I might be able to tear myself away long enough to go light another one of those things, though I could get injured and then you'd be sorry you waited."

"I am sorry," she whispered, twining her arms around his neck. "I'm sorry I said those awful things to you, that I made you wait so long, that I didn't trust and believe in you when I should have. There were some lessons I had to learn and apparently I learn best the hard way." She pressed a kiss against his chest. "I love you, Luc. So much."

"Dani, are you…?" Luc's shook his head, threw his arms around her and squeezed. "No. Never mind. I don't care why or how or when. I only care that I love you and you love me and tonight is the best night of my entire life." He kissed her long and hard, then pulled back. "You didn't say you'd marry me," he complained.

"I'll marry you," she told him. "But I hope you aren't going to be in bandages for our wedding."

"Bandages? Why would I be?" He nuzzled her neck, his lips warm and seeking.

"Because you've singed your hair." She leaned back, studied him.

Luc groaned. "And now I suppose I look like one of the Three Stooges?"

Dani shook her head. "Nope. You look like the man God sent especially for me."

Luc spent several minutes repaying her compliment in the best way he could think of—until a vehicle honking in the distance drew his attention.

"Uh-oh. I'm counting on your love to get me through this, sweetheart," he muttered, squeezing her waist, his eyes nervously panning the landscape.

"Why? What did you do?" She twisted around, saw the row of lights driving up the valley toward the Double D. "Luc, what did you do?"

"Well, I kind of mentioned to some people that I intended to besiege the Double D tonight and get you to admit you loved me." He swallowed. "I guess they came for the fireworks."

She burst out laughing. "Then, let's give them fireworks, Doc. How many have you got?"

He met her challenge by grabbing her hand and racing her down the hill. "Lots and lots," he exclaimed, kissing her. "Wanna help?"

"Of course. We'll call it our engagement party."

"I love you."

"I know." That knowledge wiggled down into the deepest crevice of her heart and carved itself a spot

there, right beside the knowledge of her Father's love.
"I love you, too."

He grinned, then handed her the torch. "Okay, here
we go."

Luc must have splurged mightily, Dani decided.
There were balls of golden sparklers, rockets that seared
upward in a hiss of energy, then exploded in resounding
booms, squiggles that twisted and twirled their way
back to earth in a dazzling array of colors. He had five
rockets on one fuse that drew *ooh*s and *aah*s from their
audience. She even heard faint applause as the big
disco-ball rockets canceled the darkness. Then there was
the series fireworks that seemed to depend one upon
another as they exploded in waves of color that ranged
from gold to green to blue to red.

"There's one left." Luc stood behind her watching
the last of the sparks die out. "Are you ready?"

"I thought we'd lit them all." Dani nodded, loving
the touch of his fingers against her skin. "I'm ready if
you are."

"I'm ready to spend the rest of my life with you."

"Me too." She stood on tiptoe to meet his kiss.

A few catcalls from above alerted them to the others.

"The natives are restless." Luc gently urged her
away. "You stand over there. I have to do this one
myself."

She stood where he pointed, waiting, wondering what
was behind that mischievous smile. "Okay, I'm ready."

He moved to a different area, lit the fuse, then
dropped the torch in a bucket of water and walked over
to stand behind her.

The fuse burned for several seconds before she saw
that it was a series of fireworks strung across and held
by poles on both ends.

"I'm not normally a very showy person," he whispered, his arms wrapping around her waist. "I get nervous. So you'd better enjoy this public spectacle while you can."

She didn't understand what he meant, until the fuse lit a series of white sparklers that dripped like rain onto the ground. As she watched, she saw letters clearly defined across the bridge of wire.

I LOVE YOU DANI.

Tears tumbled down her cheeks as she watched the waterfall of love.

"Thank you," she whispered to heaven. "Thank you."

She showed Luc her appreciation in a more tangible way.

Some time later, Gray's voice broke through the bliss that surrounded them. "Come on, you two. We're waiting."

Luc threaded his fingers through Dani's and led her up the hill. Friends and neighbors stood scattered there, and they clapped when the couple topped the ridge. Dani nestled against Luc's side as he announced their engagement. Everyone began speaking at once as they congratulated the couple. Then, one by one, they gathered up their little ones and climbed back in their vehicles to head back to their homes.

Two men remained standing in the darkness. Dani finally realized that one was Brad.

"Congratulations, Dani," he said.

His eyes seemed sincere. Perhaps she had nothing to fear from him. But then, he'd seemed like her friend before. A niggle of worry edged itself upward in her brain.

Dani almost backed away, then remembered. Trust.

She'd trusted God with Luc, how could she not trust Him to manage Brad? Was anything too difficult for God?

No.

Dani thrust out her hand.

"Thanks, Brad." She smiled to show no hard feelings.

"I need to talk to you about something," he said, letting her hand drop. "I know you don't want to listen, and I don't blame you. I treated you pretty badly."

"It doesn't matter anymore. Truly." She looped her arm through Luc's, unwilling to let anything ruin tonight. "It's all in the past."

Brad shook his head. "Actually, it isn't."

In You will I trust. Dani repeated the words over and over in her mind, waiting for him to admit his deceit.

"I made a mistake stealing your work, Dani. Sure, I got my degree, sold it and made some money. But I couldn't produce anything else half as good, and the producers were pushing me. I came here originally thinking I'd offer you a partnership, as long as I got credit for the work. I was going to copy your *Dream* play."

She stayed silent, holding on to Luc as she prayed for the strength to keep trusting her Father.

"But then I had a little visit from your Miss Winifred. She made a few rather pointed comments, and when I watched the video back at home, I began to realize just how much of yourself you'd put into that production, how deeply it touched people. I knew then that I couldn't take it." He stepped forward, handed her the video. "It's yours, Dani, and it's wonderful."

"Th-thank you." She didn't know what else to say.

"It's so wonderful that we'd like to buy it." A man

stepped forward out of the shadows, his smile wide. "I'm Peter Regan. Brad contacted me, told me I had to see your play. He was right."

Luc was silent beside her. She twisted to look at him, to see how he was taking all of this. He smiled, squeezed her hand.

"You knew?" she whispered as the truth glowed in his eyes. "When I was barking at you about deceiving me, you knew."

And yet he'd come back, set off the fireworks, waited for her.

"I'm so sorry, Luc. How can you love me?" she whispered.

"So easily." His lips brushed her hair. "You have no idea."

The Father's plans. How could she understand them? She would never understand that kind of love. And she didn't have to. But she could trust in it, find hope in it, reach out to others and show them.

"Would you be willing to sell *Three-Dollar Dream*?" Peter asked, his voice quiet. "I'd like to make it into a movie."

She frowned. It was so…personal. That play was her, it touched too close to home. Let the whole world into hers? She looked to Luc.

"Look how many people you've reached in the past three nights," he whispered. "Think how many more lives it could touch. Trust God, Dani. And trust yourself."

"I do," she told him. "I don't think I need to run away anymore."

He grinned. "A bridge across the moat?"

She grinned back, then realized they had an audience.

"This is my card. Please let me know what you decide.'' Peter handed it over. ''And thank you. I don't know when I've had such an...interesting evening.'' He grinned.

Luc laughed. ''Me, neither,'' he agreed.

''Or me,'' Brad said, and seemed surprised when Dani hugged him.

''Thanks, Brad,'' she whispered.

''You're welcome.'' He turned away quickly, but she saw the glimmer of a tear on his lashes. ''You're a special woman, Dani DeWitt.''

A moment later the two men were gone.

Luc turned so he could look into Dani's eyes.

''There's just one thing more we need to discuss tonight,'' he told her, framing her face with his palms.

''Oh?'' She stayed where she was, marveling at the work God had done in her life. ''What's that?''

''A date for our wedding.''

Dani blinked, then giggled.

''It better be soon, Doc,'' she told him. ''I don't have a home or any furniture.'' The knowledge didn't hurt a whit.

''Your home's with me, Dani. Always.''

And that was perfectly all right with her. Heaven's kiss was right here, with Luc.

Chapter Fifteen

The wedding of Dani DeWitt and Dr. Lucas Lawrence took place two weeks later in Blessing on a Saturday afternoon. Most of the town showed up for the festivities, which were ably choreographed by Miss Winifred Blessing.

The church was too small to hold everyone, so the couple were married on the church lawn, among friends, with the warm summer sun blazing down.

Dani walked down the petal-strewn aisle in her mother's wedding dress, a French silk gown she'd found while cleaning the attic. The sleek lines, fluttery skirt and off-the-shoulder bodice suited her perfectly, the white a wonderful foil for her black hair. She carried three perfect calla lilies, given by the groom as a reminder of the play that had drawn them together.

Luc wore an elegant black suit and crisp white shirt with a tiny red rosebud in the lapel, a gift from the bride whose meaning had not been explained to anyone but the groom.

The ceremony was simple, yet genuine and filled with meaning. Once it was over, folks moved to the hall where *Three-Dollar Dream* had been performed. A luncheon was spread out there for anyone who cared to eat. Most chose to take their food outside and sit amid the beauty of God's creation while they congratulated and mused over the town's newest couple.

For Dani the day could not be better. She was now Mrs. Lucas Lawrence and she loved it. If she chanced to forget, the sparkling rings on her left hand reminded her with every flicker.

Luc's hand covered hers, warm, possessive.

"Hey, Gray." He smiled at his best man.

"Before you two leave, I wanted to speak with Dani."

"Should I go?"

"No secrets, Luc." Dani held his hand tightly. "What's wrong? Adam doesn't want to run the ranch?"

"He'll run it. I'll see to that. You don't have to worry about the Double D, Dani. It's there anytime you want it back."

"Well, right now I have a husband to concentrate on," she told him with a grin. "I haven't really got time for a ranch. But I will come and visit Duke."

"Good." His sober look didn't disappear. "Marissa did some checking. In fact, she intends to keep on. But so far it looks like Fancy Dancer was exactly what you thought—a horse Dermot traded my father for land."

She laid a hand on his arm, knowing from the look on his face that he felt guilty. "Gray, use the ranch however you want. It's yours. Since the play sold, I have plenty of money. And I'd rather see someone get some benefit from it than have it abandoned. So stop feeling guilty and just be happy for us. Whatever happened in the past doesn't matter. It's the future we're looking to.''

''You're sure?'' He glanced from her to Luc and back again.

''I'm positive. I got sidetracked, put too much store in my own dreams, and not enough in God's. I've learned my lesson. The ranch is yours to use. Do with it what you will, but please leave my river section alone. Okay?''

He nodded. ''Thanks.'' He hugged her, then slapped Luc's back and slipped an envelope into his hand. ''Here's what you asked for. Enjoy.''

''Thanks, Gray. We will.''

A shower of confetti drowned them as the three Darling girls launched the last of their mother's supply.

''I think that's a sign, don't you?'' Luc waited for her nod, then glanced at Miss Winifred.

The older woman clapped her hands, drawing everyone's attention. ''The Lord and I have worked pretty hard to get these two together,'' she told them. Everyone chuckled. ''Now it's time for them to begin their married life. I know you all join me in wishing them well. Ladies, I want you to gather over here. Dani's going to throw her bouquet.''

Dani waited until they were all assembled, then tossed the charming ball of flowers, specially designed for this, over her left shoulder. A squeal of surprise greeted her. She turned, and was shocked to find that Marissa held the bouquet.

''Your aim's a little off,'' Luc teased. ''She's already married.''

"I didn't plan it that way," she laughed, poking him in the side. "It just happened."

"Nothing just happens to those who love the Lord," Miss Winifred murmured. "It's all part of His master plan."

"Just like you. Thank you, Miss Win. You've been the best friend we could have had." Dani hugged her.

"I second my wife's remarks," Luc told her. "The best."

"Thank you, dears. That being said, I hope you won't mind that I've sent along a little going-away present. Ta-ta." She scurried away, smiling.

Luc led Dani to the car and helped her inside, then got in and drove away.

"What did she mean?" he asked.

"I don't know and I don't really care. What I want to know is where we're going for our honeymoon."

Luc refused to tell her until they were at the airport. As they wafted through the air on the way to Honduras, Dani could only revel in her joy. Halfway there, the flight attendant handed them a white box.

"Compliments of Winifred Blessing," she said.

Dani looked at Luc. Together they slipped the string off the white box with the familiar red script. Inside lay a huge heart-shaped cookie with a message printed in tiny red letters.

"How did she get it so small?" Dani wondered, squinting to decipher the wording.

Love cannot be paid back. It can only be passed on.

Luc broke off a corner of the cookie and offered it to her. "She's a very smart woman, our Miss Win."

"She must approve of us going to Honduras." Dani tipped her head onto Luc's shoulder. "I always thought of it as my special place, but now I can hardly wait to share it with you.''

''You're really not upset about the ranch?''

She shook her head, all doubts gone. ''No, that's the past. I'm looking to the future.''

''So am I,'' he whispered, just before he kissed her.

* * * * *

Look for the next story in the
BLESSINGS *series*
A TIME TO REMEMBER
coming in June 2004 only from
Lois Richer and Steeple Hill Love Inspired!

Dear Reader,

Welcome back! I hope you've enjoyed this second installment in my BLESSINGS IN DISGUISE series.

Have you ever wondered what your true calling is, what it is that you were given life to do? And then, once you've settled on something, have you found yourself struggling to do it? In this day of multitasking and career change, we often struggle to climb the ladder, make an impression, to be somebody.

Dani certainly had to reevaluate her life; Luc, too. But in doing so, they both learned that humans rarely see the big picture. Isn't it reassuring to know that whatever happens to us, God uses, molds, adapts and transforms into something far beyond our expectations?

In this time of worry, fear and hurry, I wish you the peace and joy we all may find nestled in the Father's loving embrace.

Blessings to you,

Lois Richer

I'd love to hear from you.
Write me at Box 639, Nipawin, Sask.
Canada S0E 1E0 or e-mail loisricher@yahoo.com

Love Inspired®

A BABY FOR DRY CREEK

BY

JANET TRONSTAD

Reno Redfern was a dad—and he'd never even dated the baby's mother! But Chrissy Hamilton needed someone to be the father of her child, or she'd disappoint the folks back home. And the chivalrous rancher Reno was only too happy to make their pretend relationship a real one….

Don't miss

A BABY FOR DRY CREEK
On sale February 2004

Available at your favorite retail outlet.

Visit us at www.steeplehill.com

LIABFDC

Visit Steeple Hill Books online and...

EXPLORE new titles in Online Reads—
new romances every month
available only online!

LEARN more about the authors
behind your favorite Steeple Hill and
Love Inspired titles—read interviews
and more on the Authors' page.

JOIN our lively discussion groups.
Topics include prayer groups, recipes
and writers' sessions. You can find them
all on the Discussion page.

*In today's turbulent world,
quality inspirational fiction
is especially welcome, and you
can rely on Steeple Hill to
deliver it in every book.*

Steeple
Hill®

Visit us at www.steeplehill.com

SHWEB

Love Inspired ®

LOVING CARE

BY

GAIL GAYMER MARTIN

Christie Hanuman vowed to remain single…
until her ex walked back into her life a changed
man, caring for his young son and ailing father.
Patrick's newfound faith in God amazed her,
but with the history between them, could
Christie risk it all for a new happily-ever-after?

Don't miss

LOVING CARE
On sale February 2004

Available at your favorite retail outlet.

Visit us at www.steeplehill.com

LILC

TRUE DEVOTION

BY

MARTA PERRY

Pregnant and widowed, Susannah Laine needed
answers about her husband's death, and only
Nathan Sloane could provide them. But the truth
they learned threatened their budding romance.
Could God now give Susannah the strength
to overcome her past and embrace this
second chance at happiness?

Don't miss

TRUE DEVOTION
On sale February 2004

Available at your favorite retail outlet.

Visit us at www.steeplehill.com

LITD

Get to know the authors of Steeple Hill.

Among them are

HOLT WINNERS

RITA® WINNERS

READERS' CHOICE WINNERS

***ROMANTIC TIMES* REVIEWERS' CHOICE WINNERS**

BOOKSELLER'S BEST WINNERS

Do you have what it takes to become one of our home-grown best?

Visit us today at www.steeplehill.com and find out more.

Steeple Hill®

Love Inspired

SANDCASTLES

BY

JANE PEART

They were as different as cousins could be,
but Lesley, Bret and Anne had one thing in
common—the beach cottage they inherited
from their beloved grandmother. Spending
time there—alone and together—helped
the women discover what had gone wrong
in their lives…and find everlasting love.

Don't miss

SANDCASTLES

On sale February 2004

Available at your favorite retail outlet.

Visit us at www.steeplehill.com

LIS